CHOOSE YOUR WEAPONS

The big Pawnee had a tomahawk. So did Skye Fargo. It might have looked like a fair fight—but Skye knew it wasn't. The tomahawk felt clumsy in his hand. The Indian was an expert with his.

Already Skye was battered and bleeding. If the sharp edge instead of the broadside of the Pawnee's weapon had caught him, he would be dead. And he wasn't far from death now as the Pawnee closed in for the kill.

It was now or never. The Trailsman dropped his tomahawk. Which left him with his ultimate weapon and last chance: a pair of naked hands. . . .

THE TRAILSMAN
124

COLORADO QUARRY

by

Jon Sharpe

A SIGNET BOOK

SIGNET
Published by the Penguin Group
Penguin Books USA Inc., 375 Hudson Street,
New York, New York, 10014, U.S.A.
Penguin Books Ltd, 27 Wrights Lane, London W8 5TZ, England
Penguin Books Australia Ltd, Ringwood, Victoria, Australia
Penguin Books Canada Ltd, 10 Alcorn Avenue, Toronto, Ontario M4V 3B2
Penguin Books (N.Z.) Ltd, 182-190 Wairau Road,
Auckland 10, New Zealand

Penguin Books Ltd, Registered Offices:
Harmondsworth, Middlesex, England

First published by Signet, an imprint of New American Library,
a division of Penguin Books USA Inc.

First Printing, April, 1992

10 9 8 7 6 5 4 3 2 1

The first chapter of this book originally appeared in *Desert Death*,
the one hundred twenty-third volume in this series.

  REGISTERED TRADEMARK—MARCA REGISTRADA

PRINTED IN THE UNITED STATES OF AMERICA

The Trailsman

Beginnings . . . they bend the tree and they mark the man. Skye Fargo was born when he was eighteen. Terror was his midwife, vengeance his first cry. Killing spawned Skye Fargo, ruthless, cold-blooded murder. Out of the acrid smoke of gunpowder still hanging in the air, he rose, cried out a promise never forgotten.

The Trailsman they began to call him all across the West: searcher, scout, hunter, the man who could see where others only looked, his skills for hire but not his soul, the man who lived each day to the fullest, yet trailed each tomorrow. Skye Fargo, the Trailsman, the seeker who could take the wildness of a land and the wanting of a woman and make them his own.

*1860, just north of Pike's Peak
in the Colorado Territory where
enterprise and killing were
too often the same thing. . . .*

1

He was not alone in the thickly forested hills. The big man astride the magnificent Ovaro let his lake-blue eyes scan the terrain. He'd been riding the hills for most of the day when suddenly he felt it, knew it, was sure of it. More than experience, though he certainly had enough of that. Instinct, intuition, sixth sense, premonition; different people call it different things. He called it wild-creature knowing, a special kind of awareness that comes from inside someplace, not made of seeing, hearing, smelling, or touching. But every wild creature had it in varying degrees. It was as necessary to staying alive in the wild country as breathing.

He moved the horse slowly. The western kingbirds darted back and forth, flashes of gray and yellow, and the horned larks chattered. The clusters of butterfly weed were a brilliant red-orange against the dark green foliage, and box elder and hackberry grew tall. The hills seemed much the same as they had throughout the day, but now he knew someone was there. He felt it again and let his gaze sweep the land once more. This was ridged and steep-sided terrain, with deep cuts in the land below where he rode and more ridges above, all of it well-forested. He searched for a valley that was shallow and wide and ran from west and east, following the directions on the letter in his jacket pocket.

The letter had been waiting for him at Joe Benny's place when he'd finished breaking trail for Joe's cattle drive. A fat advance had been with it, and the brief note: "I need a new trail broken and word has it you're the very best—the Trailsman.'' The directions had made up the rest of it. Good money. His kind of job. He'd rested a few days in Faro's Junction with Rita Turner. It was a good few days. Rita was proof that old lovers could be friends and old friends could be lovers. The few days had been made of warm flesh, open lips and open thighs, old discoveries made new again and old ecstasies reborn.

But finally he had left, crossed into the Colorado Territory and into the high hills lush with nature's richness. He'd glimpsed bear, grizzly, herds of white-tailed deer, and plenty of muskrat and beaver. He slowed the horse again as he squinted across the hilly terrain. The Pawnee rode these hills and sometimes the Arapaho came down from the north and Kiowa from the south. But he didn't feel Indian. Didn't smell them, either, with their fish oil and bear grease mixing in with perspiration. There was something else and he had gone on for some two hundred yards more when he spotted the rider below, moving slowly in a cut of land.

He stayed on the ridge and moved the pinto forward, drawing almost parallel to the rider and halted under the branches of a thick box elder. He peered down at a slender figure, dark brown hair cut short, a tan shirt tucked into brown riding britches. He frowned as he watched the young woman lean from the saddle as she rode, plainly searching the ground for tracks. He was about to move from beneath the branches of the box elder when he caught the sound—only a moment's click of a bit chain against the bit—but his wild-creature hearing had detected it. The sound had come from above him and his eyes flicked to a ridge some two dozen yards higher up on the hillside. He saw the horseman at once, saw the man raising a rifle to his shoulder, the barrel directed down at the young woman below.

Skye Fargo frowned as he took a split second to measure distance. It was too far for accuracy with a handgun, so he reached down and pulled the big Sharps from its saddle holster. The girl had shifted direction slightly and the rifleman was still trying to line her up in his sights. Fargo brought the Sharps up, aiming with the instant precision that years had honed to a fine art. He had no idea what this was all about, why the rifleman was about to shoot the young woman. He didn't want killing, not without explanations, reasons, justification. But he saw the man was about to shoot. Fargo's finger closed on the trigger of the big Sharps and the rifle barked a fraction of a second before the man fired.

Fargo saw the man's rifle leap out of his hands as the bullet smashed into his arm just above the wrist. He fell from the far side of his horse and Fargo moved forward to look down at the young woman below. She was staring up at him and he saw her yank the six-gun from the holster at her side and fire. Two shots that whistled past his head. He ducked, but another two shots exploded, these coming closer, and he flung himself sideways from the saddle and hit the ground, rolled, came up on one knee.

"No. Hold it there, hold it!" he shouted, and broke off as another shot exploded. The shot had drowned out his call and he realized that she wouldn't listen if she'd heard him. She thought he'd taken the shot at her. He was the only one she'd seen. He rose to a crouch, moved forward, and peered cautiously over the edge of the ridge. She had leaped from her horse, the saddle empty. Two more shots echoed through the hills and sent small showers of dirt into his face. She had also reloaded. He fell backward, lay still, and cast a glance at the high ridge. The horse and the rifleman were gone, he with a bullet in his forearm. Fargo swore softly. He was left with a young woman certain he had tried to kill her. He had to try to reach her. He flattened himself on his stomach and crawled to the edge of the ridge again and peered down the slope. Nothing moved.

"Ho, down there. Listen to me," he called. "You're making a mistake. You've got it all wrong." He paused, listened and his only answer was silence. "Come out and we can talk," he said. "I'll come out, too," he tried. Again there was only silence, and he frowned as he wondered whether she had managed to sneak away. He pulled himself closer to the edge to get a better view of the bottom of the slope. The shot slammed into the dirt only an inch from his shoulder and he rolled and skittered back from the edge. "Damn," he swore aloud.

She wasn't about to believe in words and he swore again at her distrust even as he realized he couldn't blame her. Words were cheap. They all too often cloaked trickery. But he'd not stay trapped like a rabbit on the ridge by some six-gun-toting furious female. Besides, his curiosity was thoroughly aroused now. He moved back a few feet farther and let his eyes scan the ridge until he found a log, partly rotted on one side. He crawled to it, saw that it was some five feet in length. It would do perfectly. A line of dense brush and bur oak ran down the near side of the slope all the way to the bottom. Fargo pulled the log closer. From the direction of the last shot, she was lying at the very edge of the line of trees and brush, her eyes on the ridge, waiting for him to show himself again.

Fargo moved a few feet farther back at the top of the tree and brush line, lifted the log, and sent it crashing down through the trees. The foliage shook violently as the log rolled and tumbled down the slope. It sounded exactly as he'd wanted it to sound, as though someone were racing with wild abandon down the slope through the heavy brush and tree cover. He was smiling as the next sound erupted, a volley of gunshots, and he raced to the edge of the ridge. The shots were coming from inside a cluster of brush. If it had been a person crashing down the slope, one shot at least would've winged him.

Fargo counted off the shots, and when the sixth one resounded, he leaped down over the edge of the ridge and half slid, half ran down the slope to reach her before she could reload. She had just jammed the first cartridge into the gun when he reached her, and she whirled to bring the revolver up and fire. But he came in low with a flying tackle that caught her around the knees. She went down and the shot exploded harmlessly into the air. "Damn, little hellcat," he swore as he avoided a raking swipe of her nails and managed to close one hand around her wrist. He twisted and she gasped in fury and pain as the gun fell from her hand. She tried to raise a knee and sink it into his groin, but he felt her leg move and turned. She only got a piece of his outer thigh. He swore again, got his other hand on her arm, and flung her onto her back.

He was on top of her at once, holding her arms pinned against the ground. "Stop it, damn it," he rasped. Brown eyes shot fury at him out of an attractive face—a short, straight nose and even features, with lips that were no doubt nicely shaped when not biting down on each other.

"Bastard," she spat at him.

He pushed himself to his feet, yanked her up with him, and shook her as though she were a rag doll, her head snapping back and forth. "I didn't fire at you," he yelled when he stopped shaking her. "You hear me, you damn spitfire?"

She glowered back, found her breath. "Some damn squirrel did it? You were the only one up there," she said.

"No, there was someone else, on the ridge above me," Fargo said. "He had his rifle aimed for you. I wounded him to stop him."

"You expect me to believe that?" she sneered.

He took his hands from her arms. "No, you couldn't do that, could you?" he tossed back.

She flung a glance up at the high ridge. "Where is this someone else? You said you shot him."

"I said I wounded him. He got away. That was your doing," Fargo snapped.

"My doing?"

"Yes, you had me so busy dodging bullets, he got the

chance to take off," Fargo accused. Her eyes narrowed, but he saw neither fear nor acceptance in them. He had to break through her wall of skepticism. "Why aren't you dead?" he flung at her, and she met his stare. "If I tried to kill you, why haven't I finished it?" he pressed.

She glowered back. "I don't know. Maybe you're still going to. Maybe you'll take your time. Maybe you're a damn crazy," she said. "But I don't buy words, mister."

He grasped hold of her wrist and flung her forward. "Start climbing, goddammit," he growled, and she turned and started to pull herself up the slope ahead of him. He watched her as he followed, and took in a long, lean figure, a trim, tight rear, a strong back under the tan shirt that fitted tightly and breasts that seemed on the shallow side yet filling out at the bottom. They moved as she climbed, swaying with the pull of her body.

He stayed with her as they reached the middle ridge and saw her quick glance at the Ovaro, her eyes pausing on the horse's jet-black fore- and hindquarters and glistening white midsection. "Keep going," he growled, and she continued to climb up the second slope, which turned out to be somewhat steeper than the lower one. She slipped twice, caught herself and quickly recovered. There was a lithe grace in the way her lean body moved, he noted. He finally reached the high ridge with her and stepped to the left, his gaze sweeping the ground until he found what he sought. He dropped to one knee and gestured to her, pointing out first the hoofprints still clear in the soft mountain bromegrass and then the drops of blood on the ground.

She stared down, a deep furrow creasing her smooth forehead. "I'll be damned," she muttered finally. Fargo rose to his feet to fasten her with a stern glance.

"I'd say you owe me an apology, girl," he said.

"Seems that way."

"Seems?" he pressed.

"All right, it is that way," she said with a touch of defiance.

"Apologies come hard for you, don't they?"

"I'm not used to them," she admitted.

"You've a name?"

"Names don't matter," she said. "I thank you for what you did and I'm glad I missed winging you." She turned abruptly and started down the steep slope, moving carefully. He followed and caught up to her when she reached the ridge below, where the Ovaro waited.

"Hold on, dammit," he said, and she paused. "Why all the secrecy?"

"No secrecy. You did a good deed. I'm beholden to you for that. There's no need for anything more," she said, her even-featured attractiveness quietly adamant.

"This whole thing's awfully strange," Fargo muttered.

"Guess so," she said.

His eyes narrowed on her. "And you still aren't sure about me, are you?"

The young woman shrugged. "Like you said, this whole thing's awfully strange, you being here at the right moment and everything."

"Luck. Good luck for you."

"Seems that way," she said.

He looked at her hard. It was becoming obvious that she wasn't about to trust him. She was being very cautious. Maybe with good reason. Maybe she had reason to suspect more than one enemy. "Who was the man that aimed to kill you?" he asked.

"I don't know."

"And you can't even guess," he said, sarcasm in his tone.

"I didn't say that," she returned. She paused, her brown eyes studying him for a moment longer. "Look, you seem to have done me a real favor, but you're still a stranger, mister. I don't guess with strangers."

"You don't even tell them your name," he grunted.

"Mary," she said, turned, and started down the second slope to her horse. He stayed on the ridge and watched her swing into the saddle with easy grace. "Much obliged," she called up to him with a wave, and rode into the trees.

He watched her disappear and slowly walked to the Ovaro, pulled himself into the saddle, and rode on along the ridge. It had been a strangely unsettling experience, full of things left hanging, and he always disliked that. She had been unsettling, attractive yet very reserved, almost fearful. No, that wasn't the word, he corrected himself. She had too much fight in her for that word. He cast around for another and came up with distrustful, monumentally distrustful. That fitted her better. But why? he wondered. And why had someone been out to blast her with a rifle shot? She had been surprised by the fact, but not shaken and certainly not mystified.

He shook his head again. A passing incident that would likely stay unexplained. He turned his concentration back to the land as he sought the shallow valley. As he saw dusk sliding across the hills, he found a spot beneath a red cedar to camp and unsaddled the Ovaro. The hills turned cool and he made a small fire, enough to warm some beef jerky. As soon as he finished eating, he stretched out his bedroll, undressed and lay down. He went to sleep with thoughts of the strange young woman drifting through his mind.

When he woke, the chickadees filled the morning air with their quick, three-note calls, and he found a small stream to wash in and a wild plum arbor for breakfast. He rode out onto the ridge again, and followed the land as it dipped downward, high green hills staying on his right. Suddenly he caught sight of the shallow valley. He put the pinto into a trot, swung into the valley, and followed it eastward. He found that it soon narrowed and became not much more than a wide path. A lake was his next landmark, and he rode into the afternoon with the high, tree-covered land still on his right.

The terrain had become less ridged and jagged now, the hills rolling with swooping inclines well-covered with cedar, bur oak, and cottonwood. The flash of sun on blue water a few hundred yards ahead caught his eye, and he spurred the Ovaro forward along the rise of land at his right. The pleasant quiet of the day exploded with the sudden, crackling sound of a rifle shot, an out-of-place, obscene sound. He felt the shot cross inches in front of him and he flung himself from the saddle, hit the ground, and rolled into a low stretch of brush as another shot exploded. He had the Colt in his hand as his eyes peered at the rise of land across from him, letting his gaze move along the trees. He spied the foliage sway a few dozen feet from the passageway where he'd been riding.

He watched the line of the foliage as it moved. His attacker was moving down toward level ground. He waited till the foliage moved almost directly across from him. He raised the big Colt, wishing he'd had a chance to take the Sharps from its saddlecase, and fired two quick shots. The foliage stopped moving. Fargo waited and watched, but nothing swayed or rustled. Was his attacker the man he'd winged on the ridge yesterday, he wondered. It was possible. A splint on his forearm wouldn't prevent him from using a rifle. He let three minutes go by and swore softly. Maybe his two shots had both landed. A standoff wouldn't give him an answer, he knew. He had to do something to find out. He moved, rose, shook the lower branches of a young cedar, and dropped flat. Nothing happened. No rifle bullets whistled into the tree.

His eyes moved to his left, along the passageway to where it ended in a stand of red cedar, brush, and hackberry. It would give him a way to crawl to the other side and surprise someone very cagey or find someone very dead. He lay down on his stomach and began to crawl along the brush, moving slowly, almost inching his way to avoid disturbing even a leaf. He kept tossing glances across at the other side as he crawled, but caught no sign of movement. The crawling was agonizingly slow, but he forced down impatience that tried to push him into moving too fast and rustling a branch or a tree. He finally reached the place where the passageway ended and he carefully turned himself, staying flat as he began to inch his way toward the other side.

He pushed high grass from in front of his face, moved a piece of broken branch, and crawled forward again. He had reached the center of the trees that ended the passageway when he caught the flicker of movement in front of him. He lifted his head and found himself staring face to face with a figure also flattened on the ground and crawling toward him. The other figure, not more than a dozen feet away, stared back, and he saw the rifle clutched in one hand. He also saw light brown hair worn loose and shoulder-length, a short, straight nose, full cheeks and medium blue eyes that stared back at him with equal surprise.

But the moment of surprise exploded in a simultaneous reaction. He saw her press her hand into the ground and try to bring up the rifle, and he rolled, and kept rolling until he came up against the wide trunk of a red cedar. He took refuge there, the Colt in hand. "What the hell is this? Ladies day again?" he swore aloud to himself.

2

Fargo edged around the tree trunk. He could hear her in the tall brush, maybe a dozen feet away. "Dammit, why are you shooting at me, girl?" he shouted out.

"That's a dumb question, mister," she returned.

Fargo swore silently, the answer not without its own wry truth. "You've made a mistake," he tried.

"No, you have," the answer came.

He swore again. It was yesterday with variations, only even stranger. Mary whatever-her-last-name-was, had a reason for shooting at him, mistaken as it had been. She'd thought he had tried to kill her. This one wasn't about to listen to explanations, either—that was becoming very clear.

But one thing was firm in his mind. Two implacable trigger-happy females in two days was too much. Maybe there was a connection. Maybe not. Maybe these hills were full of shooting females. But he'd find out. He had to, if he wanted to escape without holes. She was in the brush, rifle raised, waiting. He had the location pretty well fixed, though she was invisible from ground level.

He went over his options. He could move quickly, pour bullets into the brush, reload fast and pour in another volley, spray shoot in a concentrated area. Some of his shots would hit on target, that was almost a certainty. But there'd be no way to give her a flesh wound, no control over death and he didn't want that. He wanted his own skin safe and some answers. He grimaced. If he had his lariat he'd have his way out but the rope was on the Ovaro's saddle. But the thought stayed with him, and offered a variation—not an easy one, but one he'd have to take.

He stepped back, reached both arms up to one of the tree's lower branches. He let his body dangle for a moment and then swung himself up and over the branch. He balanced himself on the branch and began to climb higher into the tree. He climbed slowly, each pull a careful one, each step tested first before following with all his weight. The heavy branches hardly moved and he made his way to the other side of the tree and rested himself on the crook of a branch. The young woman was almost below him, clearly visible from his perch in the tree. Using both hands, he let himself swing down to the branch below, and then the one below that. He was as low as he dared descend and he stayed motionless, poised on the branch with one leg stretched backward, the other almost kneeling.

He peered down at her again. She was frowning as she directed all her attention to the trunk of the tree. He saw her cock her head to one side to strain her ears for a sound. He carefully drew the big Colt from its holster, tensed every muscle as he took aim and then let a volley of shots fly. Emptying the chamber, he sprayed bullets in a half-circle around her. She flinched, trying to make herself smaller and reacted with surprise and terror. He leaped from the tree as he fired off the last shot, landed on both feet alongside her, knocking her over as he did. He scooped the rifle from the ground where she had dropped it and flung it into the brush. She started to recover and looked up at him, astonishment in her face. He yanked her to her feet and flung her out of the brush into the open.

She was as tall as the young woman yesterday, but with a rounder figure, higher breasts—not terribly large either but fuller. She was a shade more attractive in a more usual way, rounder cheeks, a more conventionally pretty face with none of the other young woman's lean angular looks. "Talk, dammit," Fargo bit out at her.

"Go to hell," she threw back.

He shot an arm out, grabbed her by the wrist and twisted her arm up behind her and she cried out in pain. "I've never had much patience and you've used up all of it. Talk, dammit," he demanded.

"Screw yourself," she snapped and cried out again as he twisted. "You won't get anything out of me, bastard," she choked out. He let go of her and stepped back. Short of sheer brutality, she wasn't the kind to scare or shrink from pain and he allowed her a grudging admiration. His eyes went past her to the edge of the trees and he spotted the Appaloosa just under the branches of an oak. He was pretty convinced of one thing and the horse confirmed it—no travel bags, not even a bedroll behind the saddle. Wherever she was from, it wasn't far away.

"You're going to take me home," he said and saw her eyes widen.

"Like hell I am," she snapped.

He leveled a hard stare at her. "I want some answers. I could've killed you just now, but I didn't. I'm going to give you one more chance. You tell me why you tried to blow my head off or you take me to wherever you've come from and I'll get the answers there."

"I'm not tellin' you anything and I'm not taking you anywhere," she said with an offhand defiance.

"How do you know I won't put a bullet into you right now?" he speared.

Her blue eyes searched his face. "You're not the type to kill a woman in cold blood," she said.

He paused, uttered a wry grunt. "You're right, there. Not much stomach for it," he said. "But I've no problem letting somebody or something else do it." He reached out, took her wrist and yanked her with him to the Ovaro where he took the lariat and quickly bound her wrists. He cut off another length of the rope, led her to a young tree and bound her to it, wrapping her arms and ankles tight.

"Bastard," she spit at him as he stepped back. But there was something new in her eyes, the tiniest glimmer of fear and he smiled inwardly as he walked to the Ovaro and swung onto the horse. "You can't leave me here like this. This is grizzly country," she said.

"I know. Saw a few," Fargo nodded blandly.

"Wolf country, too," she said.

"Yep," he agreed. "And don't forget about the Pawnee and the Kiowa. You ready to talk?"

"No," she snapped.

"Then I guess life's going to be a lot simpler for you, now," Fargo said and she questioned with her eyes. "All you have to think about is whether you'll be torn apart or scalped," he finished.

He walked the horse toward the line of trees and paused to look back at her. "Bastard," she flung at him.

"You change your mind, honey, you better pray I'm not too far away to hear you," he said and disappeared into the trees. He rode slowly and knew he was counting on survival winning over stubbornness, common sense over conviction. But he could be guessing wrong, he realized. He was still having trouble believing the entire incident, especially after the one yesterday. Maybe nobody in these hills used any sense. He was almost through the line of oaks, the blue of the lake clear and bright ahead of him and he drew the horse to a halt.

His lips drew back in a grimace as he wondered if he'd already pulled out of hearing. He couldn't simply return. He'd never get a damn thing out of her then. But he knew he couldn't leave her either and realized he'd boxed himself into a bit of a bind. He was deciding that he'd have to sneak back, stay out of sight and keep an eye on her when he heard the call, distant and faint. One word, "Wait." He smiled as he turned the Ovaro around. But he rode very slowly, let the horse halt to nibble on some of the soft bromegrass. Let her think she'd waited too long, he told himself. It might loosen her tongue. But he finally pushed his way through the trees into the clear land of the passageway and saw the moment of relief flare in her eyes, only to be quickly extinguished by a glare.

'It took you long enough,'' she snapped.

"You're lucky. I almost didn't hear you,'' he said, dismounted and untied her. He watched her swing onto the Appaloosa, anger and resentment in her face. But an acceptance, at last temporarily. He brought the Ovaro alongside her, a half step behind. "I like to know who I'm riding with,'' he said.

"Bonnie,'' she muttered.

"That's all?''

"That's enough.''

He shrugged but didn't press her further. First names only seemed to be the custom in these parts, he grunted, thinking of the young woman yesterday. He took in Bonnie as she rode. She sat her horse well, her figure sturdy. "You could maybe save us both a lot of trouble if you tell me who you are and what this is all about,'' he ventured.

"Don't try to sweet-talk me, mister. You know what it's about,'' she returned.

He shrugged and decided not to press her further, confident he'd have some answers soon. He marked the route in his mind as they rode, every little detail imprinting itself in his mind, shapes and stones, trees and turns, all becoming sentences for future use. It was second nature to him, as automatic as breathing. He was the land and the land was him— the Trailsman. When they came within sight of a house set in the hollow, the way to it became indelibly stamped inside him.

The house was a modest, sturdy woodframe. He noticed two small corrals nearby, only a few horses in each, mostly quarterhorses but he spied an Appaloosa mare. As they reached the front of the house, Fargo saw the young woman's body tense, subtle changes in the way she sat the horse, her thighs tightening, her heels starting to pull back in the stirrups. She was going to make a move, maybe sound an alarm and his hand slid over the butt of the big Colt at his side. He was ready and waiting when she made her move.

"Shoot him," she screamed and started to fling herself back over the Appaloosa's spotted rump. But she felt the Colt jammed into the small of her back before she had a chance to reach the horse's rump. She froze. "Don't shoot him," she called out.

"That's better," Fargo growled.

She sat still with the Colt in her back as the front door of the house opened and Fargo saw the figure step out, rifle in hand, short, dark-brown hair and a lean, tight body wearing a tan shirt and brown riding britches. "I'll be damned," he breathed. "You. I think you said the name was Mary."

The young woman lowered the rifle and peered at the girl on the Appaloosa with a frown. "What the hell did you bring him here for?" she spit out.

"I didn't exactly bring him," Bonnie snapped back. "You know him?"

"He's the one I told you about yesterday," Mary said.

Fargo felt the irritation spiral inside him as he pulled the Colt from the girl's back and fastened his eyes on the other young woman. "She tried to blow my head off. You want to tell me why? You send her, dammit?"

"No, I didn't send her," the young woman flared and brought her eyes to Bonnie. "Dammit, I told you you can't just go around shooting at people," she said sternly.

"I figured he had to be one of them coming to try and sneak up on us," Bonnie said.

"One of who?" Fargo cut in.

"Never mind," Bonnie threw at him as she slid from the Appaloosa and faced the other girl. "I mean, who else would be riding through here?" she said.

"Anybody passing through, dammit," Fargo answered.

"He's right," Mary said. "That's why I warned you about going off half-cocked. You can't jump to conclusions."

"And we can't let a ringer sneak up on us," Bonnie countered.

"Look, I hate to interrupt an argument but who the hell are you two? And why are you so all-fired anxious to shoot at people?" Fargo questioned.

"That's not your concern," Mary said. "Just what are you doing here in the hills, mister?"

"I'm on my way somewhere, not that it's any of your business," Fargo answered harshly and eyed the two young women. They were very different physically, except both had short, straight noses and were attractive. But there was more similarity to them, not just their attitude of distrustful belligerence, but a kind of shared intensity, as if both were fed by the same fires. "I'd still like knowing what you two are so worried about that you shoot without even a second thought," he said.

"We've our reasons," Mary said. "You just go your way and forget you ever met up with us."

"That'll take a while," he grunted.

"Work on it," Bonnie said. "I'm sorry about the mistake." He saw her eyes move up and down his powerful frame. "I really wouldn't want to shoot anything as good-looking as you."

"Stable your horse," Mary cut in with obvious annoyance and the young woman led the Appaloosa away. But not before Fargo caught her giving him a last glance and a tiny smile edging her lips. "You'll have to excuse Bonnie. She's always had a bold streak in her with men," Mary said stiffly.

"I'll take being screwed over being shot," Fargo said and received cold disapproval.

"You can go your way now," Mary said, with ice in her eyes.

"Still no names?" Fargo tried.

"No need yesterday, none today," the young woman said and he saw Bonnie return, the tiny hint of a smile still on her lips.

"Maybe some other time, some other place," Bonnie said.

"Maybe," Fargo nodded to her and turned the Ovaro in a circle and paused to glance back at the two young women. "There any more like you in these hills?" he asked. "I don't hanker on being a target again."

"No," Bonnie said and he walked the horse away. But his eyes swept the barn and the corrals and took in an old gatepost as he searched for a name, an initial, a mark, anything he could take with him to inquire about. But there was nothing and he put the pinto into a trot, rode a slow slope and the house disappeared from view behind him.

He retraced his steps till he reached the spot where Bonnie had tried to let daylight through him. From there he rode on, circled the lake and found the road marked in the note in his pocket. The two young women stayed in his mind, a damn unusual pair indeed. They were both too young to be called spinsters, and both were too intense to be distaff hermits withdrawn from the world. They weren't withdrawn from anything. They were on guard and belligerent and something more. He'd picked up strange emanations from the pair, a driving intensity that made it hard to dismiss them as simply a pair of crazies. But that was a possibility, he had to admit as he rode on, knowing his curiosity would make him inquire further.

He pushed aside thinking more about the two young women and followed the road to a twin-peaked boulder, turned into a hollow of land and soon the ranch came into sight; a large house with a big spread, at least four main corrals where cowpunchers were working with horses. Fargo rode up to the long, low main house, heavy-timbered and saw a long, wide enclosure with wire on all sides and a wire gate. At first, he thought the animals he saw inside the wire compound were wolves, at least a dozen of them. Then he realized they were dogs, large German shepherds, gray-black with brown markings. Another half-dozen dogs appeared, perhaps mixed breeds or breeds he'd never seen before.

The dogs watched him with steady, calm eyes, no snarling or barking. They were plainly very well-trained. He heard the door of the house open and turned to see a burly figure, the man's short-cropped mustache and short hair adding to his square-faced appearance. Fargo saw gray eyes, a little on the hard side, appraise him with polite wariness. "Horace Gregory?" Fargo asked.

"That's right," the man said in a gravelly voice.

"Fargo—Skye Fargo. I believe you sent for me," the Trailsman said and saw Horace Gregory's face break open in a hearty grin.

"Welcome. Been waiting for you, Fargo," the man said. "Wasn't sure if you were going to take my traveling advance."

"Never turn down a job without listening," Fargo said.

"I see you're interested in my puppies," Horace Gregory said with a hearty laugh.

"Some puppies," Fargo commented, eyeing one of the hundred-pound shepherds. His glance went to three of the other dogs, smaller, about sixty pounds, he guessed, with moderately long coats of black and white and some with gray-merle ticking. "Crossbreeds?" he inquired.

"No, sir. Those are Australian border collies. I imported two litters and bred more myself," Horace Gregory said pridefully. "The other three big ones with the black and brown coats and white fronts are Bernese mountain dogs."

"You're a dog fancier," Fargo said.

"A hobby. Mostly I'm into other business. Horses, for one. Let's go inside where we can relax while we talk," the man said and Fargo followed him into a large living room, furnished with chairs and a long sofa, the walls bare except for two rifles. It was, Fargo decided, a room that cried out for better, classier furnishings. "Drink?" Horace Gregory asked as he paused at a cabinet.

"Bourbon, if you have it," Fargo said. The man nodded and brought out a bottle of Bardstown bourbon that was rich and smooth. Fargo savored his first sip as he lowered himself into a hardbacked chair. Horace Gregory deposited his burly body on a wooden bench and took a deep draw of his drink.

"I sent for you because I want you to find the best trail through these hills going west," the man said. "Nothing that needs fit a cattle drive. I only need a trail wide enough for a horse and rider. But I want a trail that'll let a rider make time straight through the hills."

"I'm a curious man by nature," Fargo said.

"I'm going to open a new mail route. I figure if I can get a fast trail right through these hills I'll have a real advantage," Horace Gregory said. "Your job will be to find it, map it out for me so's I can make copies for my riders. Once they ride it a spell, they won't need a map, of course."

"I never take a man's money for nothing. I'd like to look around a little more. Sometimes in hills such as these there just isn't the kind of trail you'll need. I expect there is, but I want to be sure," Fargo said.

"Fair enough," the man agreed.

"And I'm wondering what else is going on around here," Fargo remarked.

"What makes you wonder that?" Horace Gregory asked.

"I damn near had my head blown off on the way here. Twice," Fargo said.

"You see who tried?" Horace Gregory asked.

"Sure did. Two gals, one yesterday, the other today," Fargo said.

"Jesus, you ran into the Keegan cousins," Gregory said and drained his drink. "Goddamn crazy females, both of them."

"Mary and Bonnie?"

"That's right," the man said and his face grew hard, his jaw tight. "They just tried to dry gulch you?"

"One of them did that," Fargo said. "But it was plain that they both thought I might be somebody else."

"They tell you who?" the man questioned.

"No."

"They tell you anything about themselves?"

"Not a word."

"They mention my name?" Gregory pressed.

"No," Fargo said as the man's gray eyes stayed hard. He was plainly upset, Fargo noted and decided to try a question himself. "Why would they be mentioning your name?"

"They don't like the idea of my running a mail route through these hills," Horace Gregory said. "They're crazy. They think the damn hills are theirs."

"They seemed real afraid of something," Fargo said.

"They sit in that old house and make up all kinds of wild stories. It's all in their imaginations," the man said.

"Not all of it," Fargo said and drew a frown from Horace Gregory. "Somebody was going to kill Mary Keegan. I saw him."

"You saw him?"

"That's right. He'd have done it if I hadn't happened to be there and winged him," Fargo said.

"Guess she's lucky for that," the man said.

"You know why somebody was out to shoot her?" Fargo asked.

"No, but it doesn't surprise me any. They've made so many enemies with their crazy ways, including plenty of folks in Hillsdale," Gregory said. Fargo frowned inwardly. He'd passed through Hillsdale where it nestled at the foot of the high hills. A very ordinary town with its biggest attraction the dance hall. He wondered who Mary and Bonnie Keegan could alienate there. "No matter," Gregory's voice broke into his thoughts. "You can forget about the Keegan cousins. They'll be no concern of yours."

"Guess not," Fargo said, finished the bourbon and got to his feet. Horace Gregory walked outside with him and Fargo saw the dogs immediately rush to the wire fencing at Gregory's appearance. "They like you," he commented.

"Sure. I trained them all," the man said.

"I'll be getting back to you," Fargo said as he swung onto the Ovaro.

"Soon. I'm anxious to get going with my mail route. Already got government approval to carry the mail when I'm ready," Gregory said.

"Soon," Fargo promised. Horace Gregory and his German shepherds watched him ride away.

Darkness was moving in quickly, he saw, perhaps another half hour of daylight left. He rode back to the lake, found a spot to bed down under a peachleaf willow and watched the moon rise across the water as he ate from the beef jerky in his saddlebag. The two young women had proper names now. Mary and Bonnie Keegan. His talk with Horace Gregory stayed in his mind. The man had dismissed the two young women with contempt, yet he'd been awfully anxious about what they might have said about him. His questions had come with rapid-fire speed, more than simple curiosity behind them. A hint of alarm, Fargo recalled.

The Keegan cousins had told him almost nothing. Perhaps Horace Gregory had told him less than the truth. But another question pushed itself at him. Mary and Bonnie Keegan, for all their short-fused tempers, had been fearful and on guard. And somebody had tried to kill Mary. Those were facts that begged knowing more about and as he undressed and lay on his bedroll, he decided to pursue the unexplained a little further. Finding a trail for a new mail route was one thing. Riding into a hornet's nest was another.

3

When morning came, he found a small stream in which to wash and a stand of wild plums and blackberries for breakfast. First things first, he reminded himself and spent the rest of the morning exploring the high hill country with practiced eyes. He paused atop ledges and ridges, peered westward and nosed the pinto through the beginnings of a half-dozen deer trails. Finally satisfied that there were trails to be found running more or less straight through the hills, he turned the horse and slowly rode toward where the Keegan house sat in the small hollow.

He kept the pinto in the heavy tree cover and edged closer from one side, not approaching from the front. He saw Bonnie come from the house to fetch water from the well, clad only in a skirt and the top of her slip. The modest but high round breasts swayed as she bent low over the well. He took in nicely rounded shoulders, a firm upper body with a slightly barrel-chested ribcage. He edged the pinto out of the trees and came up to her from the side just as she had the bucket filled. She whirled with surprise in her eyes, her mouth falling open.

"Damn," she murmured. The door of the house flew open and Mary emerged, rifle in hand to stare at him with equal surprise.

" 'Afternoon, ladies," Fargo said pleasantly and swung from the pinto.

"You found your way back here," Bonnie said. "I'll be damned."

"It wasn't very hard to do," Fargo said. "Besides, that's why they call me the Trailsman."

Mary stepped forward and set the rifle against the door but she peered at him with a frown. "The Trailsman. I heard Horace Gregory hired somebody special to find him his route," she slid at him.

"You heard right," Fargo said. "The name's Fargo—Skye Fargo."

"You're the one he hired," Mary said, her eyes boring into him and he nodded.

"Dammit, I told you we should've shot him," Bonnie said. "Good looks and all."

Fargo let his eyes move calmly from her to Mary and back again. "Bonnie and Mary Keegan," he said. "The Keegan cousins. You see, you do have names."

"Get out of here. Nobody part of Horace Gregory's operation comes on our land," Bonnie said.

"Back off, honey," Fargo said harshly. "I'm not part of Horace Gregory's operation. He hired me to do the special kind of job I do best."

"Then do it and leave us alone. You've no need to come around here," Mary glowered.

"I came to hear what you had to say. Maybe you ought to simmer down some and behave like ladies, though that may be asking too much," he said.

"Go to hell," Mary muttered.

He smiled. "In due time. Meanwhile, I'm here. Why don't you tell me what you've got against Horace Gregory's mail route through these hills?"

"It's not just the mail route. It's him. You saw that he sent somebody to kill me," Mary said.

"I saw a man about to do that. I don't know who sent him. Maybe he came on his own. According to Gregory, you two have made a lot of enemies, including folks in Hillsdale,"

Fargo said and saw the quick exchange of glances between the two young women.

"That's got nothing to do with Gregory," Mary said.

"It's got to do with enemies," Fargo said and she shrugged. "Maybe you're blaming the man for things you shouldn't."

"Horace Gregory's no damn good," Mary shot out with a burst of fury. "And his mail route is nothing but a cover to let him rustle horses."

"Rustle horses?" Fargo frowned.

"Yes. It'll give him a legitimate reason to send a man riding through the hills at all hours to spot where folks have their horses and the best time to rustle them," Mary said. "Hell, he's doing it now. He just wants to expand his operation with a rider nobody can stop or even challenge. Hell, he'll be carrying U.S. Mail."

"You have horses he's rustled?" Fargo asked and they both nodded. "But you've no proof against him," Fargo pressed.

"We know," Bonnie said.

"You suspect. You think. You've no proof, that's what it comes down to," Fargo said. "And you could be all wrong about his mail route, too."

"Dammit, we're not wrong. It's a damn excuse," Mary said. "Come inside." She turned and strode into the house and Fargo followed, Bonnie falling in step beside him. She took a shirt from a wall peg and slipped it on.

"I don't want you getting too excited," she tossed at him.

"That makes two of us," Fargo returned as he took in a modest living room: two sofas and a round table and straight-backed chairs. There were curtains on the windows, a tablecloth on the main table and another smaller one, doilies atop a bureau—more feminine than he'd expected. "What are you two doing up here on your own?" he asked.

"Our grandpa raised us. When he died, he left us everything, meaning the house and land," Bonnie said. "And enough money to live. Grandpa made it with a silver mine years ago."

Mary, standing by the main table, peered at a map laid out on it and beckoned to Fargo. He came to stand beside her. She pointed to a spot on the map. "This is where we are, these hills. Just above us there's the Leavenworth and Pike's Peak Express Line and just below us, here, is the Butterfield Overland Despatch that runs along the Smoky Hills trail," she said. "You see any damn reason for another mail route through these hills?"

Fargo's eyes stayed on the map for a long moment before he pursed his lips. "No, I can't say that I do," he admitted and Mary uttered a snort of triumph.

"Exactly. There isn't any. Gregory's mail route is nothing but a cover," she said.

"Now, hold on," Fargo said. "The fact that I can't see a reason, and you don't see a reason, doesn't mean there isn't one. Maybe there are things we don't know. Maybe the Butterfield Overland Despatch is doing a poor job, or the Leavenworth line is."

"We checked. They're both running fine," Bonnie said.

Fargo shrugged. "The bottom line is that a man's got a right to run an express mail line if the government agrees to let him carry mail. If he's picked a poor route, and nobody sends mail with him, he'll go out of business."

"Only Horace Gregory doesn't give a damn about that," Mary said. "He only wants a cover to rustle horses, I tell you."

"You admit you've no proof he does that," Fargo said.

"He's real clever," Bonnie put in.

"Then somebody's going to have to be more clever to catch him at it," Fargo said and eyed the two young women carefully. "Tell me about Hillsdale," he said.

"Abe McAdoo runs the dance hall. We met some of his girls and found out how little he was paying them and how badly he was treating them. We got them all to quit on him

36

until he agreed to change his ways. He was real mad at us. So were a lot of his customers," Mary said.

"Was?" Fargo inquired.

"All right, still is. It wasn't that long ago," Mary conceded.

"Seems you two have a wide streak of the reformer in you," Fargo commented.

"We don't like to see anybody hurt when there's no reason, two-legged or four-legged," Bonnie said.

"All this doesn't change the fact that Horace Gregory can open a mail route," Fargo said.

"And you're going to break a trail for him to do it," Mary said.

"I agreed. He paid me advance money. I keep my word," Fargo said. "I sure as hell won't break it on account of wild talk without real proof."

"Then you can leave now," Mary said. Fargo shrugged and walked from the house, aware of both young women following him outside. He climbed onto the Ovaro and swept them with a glance.

"Sorry," he said. "Somebody tried to kill you, Mary Keegan. I know that. But you've no proof Horace Gregory had anything to do with it. Your own words admit it could've been a lot of people. Maybe I'll come visit again when I'm finished."

"Don't bother." Mary said and glared and Bonnie remained silent. He turned the Ovaro and rode from the house, moving up the steep slope. A strange pair. That first impression had only been strengthened. But a feeling of sympathy had been added. They almost invoked it. They were full of anger and accusation and wildeyed temper, and yet there seemed a kind of bruised integrity, as though they were avenging angels in tattered armor. But he had a job to do, good money waiting and that was reality. They were full of wild stories.

He had just crested a low ridge, when he heard the sound

of hoofbeats coming fast behind him. His hand dropped to the butt of the Colt at his side when he spotted the rider, shoulder-length dark brown hair blowing in the wind. But he kept his hand on the Colt. He'd sampled their tempers. Bonnie Keegan drew to a halt and slid from the Appaloosa at once, her eyes on him. When he stayed on the pinto, she curled a chiding smile at him. "I won't bite you," she said.

He returned her sarcasm as he dismounted. "Too bad," he commented and her blue eyes studied him speculatively.

"You said you were for hire," she slid at him. He nodded slowly. "We'll hire you not to find a mail route for Horace Gregory," she said as her eyes searched his face, a tiny glint in their blue depths, almost amusement.

"Mary knows you're here?" he asked.

"No, but she'll back me on it," Bonnie Keegan said. "We'll match whatever he's paying you."

"That'd just be exchanging money, yours for his. Sorry, not interested," Fargo said.

"Money's all he has to offer," Bonnie said. "We've more," she said, the tiny glint of amusement brighter now.

Fargo smiled at her. "You talking for Mary, too?" he asked.

"No, for myself," she said. "Don't be greedy."

"Just curious. But I told you. I made an agreement. I don't go back on my word," Fargo said.

She stepped toward him, a boldness in her walk, hips slightly forward, shoulders thrust back making the high, modest breasts stand forward. "Let's not play games, Fargo," she said.

"Meaning what?"

"Meaning I never saw a man who'd put a promise before pussy," she said.

"Now you have," he said blandly and saw the tiny furrow come between her eyes as she peered hard at him.

"I do believe you mean that," she murmured. He let his

silence answer. Her lips pursed as her eyes stayed on him. "What if I dropped the connection?" she said.

"That'd be different. Only it's there now. You can't separate it," he said.

"How do you know I can't?" she challenged.

"How do I know what a bobcat can do? It's called knowing the nature of the beast. Experience, honey." He laughed.

She turned and lowered herself onto a stump and he recalled how beautifully rounded her shoulders had been in the slip. "I guess that's my loss, then," she said.

"You said it yesterday. Maybe another time, another place," he remarked.

"So I did," Bonnie muttered unhappily.

He turned at the sound coming up the slope. "Seems we're going to have company," he said.

Bonnie Keegan made a face and was on her feet when Mary rode up. There was anger in the glance Mary gave her cousin and then Fargo. She returned her eyes to Bonnie.

"I expected you'd follow him," Mary Keegan snapped. "Dammit, Bonnie, you shouldn't have."

"Nothing happened," Fargo said. "You didn't give us time."

"Don't be crude," Mary said disapprovingly and turned to Bonnie again. "Go on back. It's your day for chores," she ordered and Bonnie swung onto the Appaloosa.

"You coming back?" Bonnie asked.

"In time," Mary said.

"You won't get anywhere with him," Bonnie muttered.

"I'll try my way—mind not body," Mary sniffed. Bonnie put the horse into a canter and rode away. Mary turned to see Fargo watching her. "I'm thinking maybe if you see things for yourself you'll feel differently," she said.

"Maybe, then maybe not."

"You willing to try?"

"Why not?" he answered.

"It'll be dark in an hour. We can take up a position and wait. You'll see the horses being rustled for yourself," she said.

"What makes you think it'll be tonight?"

"It's been quiet almost a week. It's time," she said and moved the horse along the ridge. He fell in beside her as she led the way. "Our horses aren't the only ones being rustled. You can talk to Will Stedman," Mary Keegan said. "His spread is due west. You can't miss if it you go that way."

"Maybe I'll visit him," Fargo said. "I don't doubt there might be horse rustling going on. I don't think you've any proof Horace Gregory's a part to back your wild ideas on why he wants to open a mail route."

"You'll see," Mary sniffed.

He watched the dusk settle over the hills. She finally pulled to a halt where the ridge broadened into a small plateau and the land on one side was a steep slope down into a long valley. Fargo peered down at the two herds of horses still visible in the dusk: one herd just below where he halted and the other further away down the valley. "That's where they are now. But he'll find them and run them off. No matter where they go, he finds them," Mary said.

Fargo turned a frown on her. "Hell, you make it easy to have them rustled. Why don't you corral them at your place?" he asked.

"Our corrals aren't big enough and we like to let them run loose. It's better for them," she said quickly, with just a touch of defensiveness.

"It's better for rustlers, too," Fargo grunted and watched the horses for a few minutes longer as the last of the light began to fade away.

"Shall we go down?" Mary asked. "I'm not for trying to ride down this slope after dark."

"No, that'd be real dangerous. But we stay here. If you're right and rustlers come, they'll ride through the valley. Down there they'd see just the two of us. From up here, we can lay down a volley of shots. You don't even have to aim. They won't know how many are shooting at them and they'll take off. Rustlers don't want gunfights which could get them caught.''

Mary nodded but tossed him a sidelong glance. "What if we don't hear them?''

''We can't help but hear them. The sound will come right up from below us,'' Fargo said.

"You'll see,'' she sniffed.

The light faded away and night plunged the land into blackness. He moved the Ovaro back from the edge of the slope and dismounted. He'd noted a big bur oak and he settled down with his back against the trunk. Mary, an almost invisible form, stretched out on the ground near him and finally took on shape as the half-moon rose to bathe her in its silver-gray light. She lay on he back, he saw, arms behind her head and her breasts had a long, lovely sweep of line. She turned her head to him as she felt his eyes on her. "Go on, ask,'' she said.

"What makes you think I've something to ask?'' he smiled.

"I can feel it,'' she said. "Anyway, most folks do.'' He smiled again, her words admitting the question hadn't been pure intuition.

"I'm curious. Who's oldest, you or Bonnie?'' he asked.

"I'm one year older and ten years wiser,'' she answered.

"And a little less than modest,'' he said.

"Bonnie would agree,'' Mary Keegan said matter-of-factly.

"Two attractive young women stuck up here in these hills,'' he said. "Why?''

"We've things that are important to us that others might not call important,'' Mary said. "Besides, you're really wondering about our social life.''

"That's part of it,'' Fargo admitted.

"We have what we want when we want it. We go into

Hillsdale and come autumn there are always harvest dances and hoedowns and quilting bees in the winter. Not in the hills but just east where the land had been settled," Mary said. "We pick and choose. Nothing wrong about that."

"No, nothing wrong about that," Fargo echoed. They were still a strange mixture but becoming more understandable—two young women with unorthodox ideas dedicated to doing things their own way. "If anything happens, we'll hear it and it won't be till later. I'm going to catch some shut-eye," he said and settled himself more comfortably against the tree trunk.

"Maybe I'll do the same," Mary said, turning on her side. He watched her breasts press into the shirt. He closed his eyes and soon heard the sound of her even breathing as she fell asleep. He let himself doze, woke twice, then fell asleep again.

The night drifted deeper when he suddenly snapped awake as the sound came from the valley below. Horses, galloping at full run. Fargo leaped to his feet and yanked the big Sharps from its saddle case. He had reached the edge of the slope and glimpsed Mary bringing her rifle to join him. But the frown dug into his brow as he peered down into the valley.

He saw no riders driving horses, heard no shouts or gunshots. All he saw was the herd of horses racing down the far end of the valley, no rustlers giving chase and none hanging back to round up stragglers. He watched the last of the herd disappear down a curve in the valley and swore softly. There was no way to give chase along the ridge. The brush and tree growth was too thick to let him catch up and sliding down the steep slope too dangerous in the dark. "I told you," he heard Mary say.

"It doesn't fit," Fargo bit out. "Maybe they haven't been rustled at all. Maybe they just took off on their own."

"All of a sudden? A whole herd just up and running away?" Mary questioned and he swore again. She was completely right. The explanation didn't hold. "Somehow, he sneaks up and runs them off," she said.

"That doesn't hold, either," Fargo said. "You can't rustle horses in silence. You have to make noise, shouting or shooting, something to set them off in the direction you want."

"Only there wasn't any of that. We didn't hear a thing. That's the way it's been every time," Mary said.

"Ghost rustlers. Phantoms," Fargo said. "I don't buy that."

"Then help us. Don't find Gregory's mail route. Find out what he's doing and how," Mary said.

"No. I keep my word. And the truth is, nothing's happened to connect Horace Gregory with anything. It's still possible that something set off your horses, spooked them and they took off," Fargo said.

"They're spooked with regularity, then," Mary said stiffly.

"Look, there's probably some reasonable explanation for what's spooked your horses. Maybe I can look into it after I've finished what I've agreed to do," Fargo said.

"You'll have given Horace Gregory his mail route then," Mary said and he shrugged.

"That's the best I can do," he said.

"I think you can do better," she said. She stepped forward and suddenly her arms were around his neck and her lips pressed hard against his. He felt the tip of her tongue slide forward, withdraw at once, but her lips clung a moment longer, softly firm. He smelled a faint scent of wintergreen on her. His lips parted, responded and his hand came up to close around her shoulder when she broke off the kiss and stepped back. A faint smile touched her lips, he saw.

"You said Bonnie had a bold streak in her with men," Fargo reminded her.

"That's right. She'd have gone on, given it all to you.

That's bold. All you get from me now is that sample and a promise," Mary said.

"That's no less bold, only a little shrewder," Fargo said. She shrugged and strode to her horse. He climbed onto the Ovaro and rode alongside her in silence until they reached her place.

"There's extra room if you want to stay and finish the night out," she said with· a truculent politeness.

"Thanks, but I'll be moving on," he said and waited while she stabled her horse and returned. "I'm sorry about your horses running off, whatever the reason," he said.

"Not sorry enough, though," she snapped and hurried into the house. He kept the Ovaro at a trot as he left. He rode across two slopes and found a low-branched box elder to bed down beside. The strange events of the night clung as he lay on his bedroll. Phantom rustlers, he grunted. Impossible, yet he had no other answer. He was becoming more and more convinced that the herd had simply been spooked.

But Mary had claimed that was the way it always happened. They were spooked with regularity, she had told him. But that didn't dismiss his thinking. Fargo frowned. Some horses were just spooky. It took very little to set them off and that could happen often enough to make it appear regular. Dammit, they'd have to bring their horses into a corral, whether they liked it or not. He had little patience for misguided stupidity. He closed his eyes and thoughts drifted away and he found sleep, waking only when the sun threw its warm caress over him.

He rose, washed at a mountain pond and breakfasted in a cluster of apple trees, enjoying the bright red and crisp taste of Jonathans and the sweet-tasting, dark red Sheepnose. He rode at an unhurried pace and it was afternoon when he reached the Gregory spread. His gaze swept the ranch as he rode in and saw that the four corrals were well filled with horses. But they had been that way during his first·visit. If they held new horses he found it impossible to tell. His eyes went to the wire compound where he saw Horace Gregory inside. The man was feeding the dogs, dishing out food into individual tin bowls with a cowhand helping him. When Gregory saw Fargo, he left his assistant to finish the feeding and emerged with a wave and a hearty grin.

"Been waiting for you, Fargo," he said. "You get your answers?"

"Yes. I can find a mail route for you," Fargo said. "Got a few other answers, too. Paid a visit to the Keegan cousins."

Horace Gregory's eyebrows lifted. "You're a glutton for punishment?" the man asked.

"Curiosity," Fargo said. "They say your mail route is a cover for you to rustle horses."

Gregory looked aghast. "Jesus, what damn fool thing will they come up with next. I told you, they're both crazy. They sit up there and dream up all kinds of wild stories."

"Not completely wild. I saw some of their horses rustled last night," Fargo said.

"You saw what?"

"A herd of their horses ran off. Damnedest thing I ever saw—no riders, no noise, nothing. But the herd was rustled," Fargo said.

Horace Gregory leaned a slep closer with a ridge across his forehead. "Their horses? In the valley a half-dozen miles south of their place?" he questioned.

"That's right," Fargo nodded.

"My friend, they don't have any damn horses. Those are all mustangs," Horace Gregory said.

Fargo felt his own forehead furrow. "Wild horses?"

"Every last one of them," the man said. "They don't have any damn horses. They sold you a cock-and-bull story. But you're not the first one they've done that to."

Fargo held the rising surge of anger inside himself. "I'll be breaking the mail route trail for you, now," he said to Horace Gregory. "I've paper and pencils enough to set down a map for you. I'll try for a line right through the middle of the hills and away from as much high land as I can."

"Fine," Gregory beamed and Fargo sent the pinto forward with a nod. He glanced back as he left the spread to see Horace Gregory playing with a half dozen of his German shepherds behind the wire of the compound. Fargo rode on and his mouth was set in a harsh, tight line as he turned the pinto north. There were too many damn strange things and conflicting stories in these hills, he muttered inwardly. He'd get an answer to at least one before he went off to break a trail for Horace Gregory. He kept the Ovaro at a steady trot until he reached the beginnings of the valley. He slowed, put the pinto into a walk and edged his way past a stand of cottonwoods along the valley floor. He'd gone perhaps a quarter of a mile when he saw the horses, grazing and wandering.

A big dun-colored stallion caught scent of him and Fargo saw his head go up. He neighed and the other horses were tensely alert at once. Fargo carefully moved closer and let his eyes scan the soft soil where the hoofprints were clear. All unshod, he saw grimly and he moved more boldly toward the herd. Under the stallion's lead they bolted at once and Fargo watched them go, all unquestionably wild horses.

He swore under his breath as he turned the pinto up a slope. He found a deer trail and followed it upward until he reached the high land and then rode west across the ridges. The Keegan place came into view and he saw Bonnie outside hanging wash behind the house. She halted and came around to meet him as he rode up. Then he saw Mary come from the house, a slight swagger to her walk.

"Expected you'd be out finding a mail route," she said.

"I will be, you can be sure of that," Fargo bit out. "I just wanted the pleasure of telling you that I found out you're a pair of lying little bitches."

He saw their eyes narrow. "What's biting at you?" Mary questioned.

"Your horses. Your horses that were rustled. You have no damn horses. Those were all wild mustangs, all of them," he flung at them and saw their exchange of quick glances. They returned their eyes to him and he found himself growing even angrier. He'd expected shame, embarrassment, perhaps an apology, but all he saw was a mild sheepishness and an almost offhanded admission.

"All right, we stretched the truth some," Mary said.

"Stretched the truth?" Fargo shouted. "Jesus, you lied your damn heads off. You accused a man of rustling horses when he's only rounding up mustangs. What the hell is it with you two?"

"That doesn't change Gregory's mail route. It's still a cover to let him find more horses," Mary said.

"Goddammit, there's no law against that. There's no law says a man can't drive wild horses. That's not rustling, dammit."

"And there's no law says we can't protect them," Bonnie put in.

"You're walking a damn thin line. You interfere with his right to drive wild horses and he can shoot you," Fargo said.

"He interferes with our right to protect them and we'll shoot him," Mary said, dogged stubbornness in her voice.

"You being stupid on purpose?" Fargo flung at her. "He's got the right to drive wild horses. Anybody does. There's no law that gives you the right to protect them."

"Some laws aren't written by men," Mary said. "Those are the ones that really count."

"Amen and hallelujah," Fargo groaned. "That won't stand up with a judge or a marshall."

"We don't give a damn about judges or marshalls. Horace Gregory's no damn good. He rounds up these beautiful animals to sell to an even bigger bastard named Rossand who has them killed and sold for meat," Mary said.

"Sold for meat? To who and where?"

"We don't know that yet."

"But we've met people who have bought horsemeat from some of Rossand's men," Bonnie said.

"Which could've come from anywhere. You're still all talk," Fargo said.

"We did some other checking. Gregory never shows up at the horse auctions with stock to sell. Never. So we know he's not breaking and selling the horses at the market. He's selling them to Rossand to be butchered, damn him," Mary said.

Fargo thought for a moment. They had their own sideways manner of coming to conclusions, yet not entirely dismissable. "If Horace Gregory's rustling horses he's a phantom rustler," Fargo said and drew glares from both young women.

"Maybe so, but he's doing it, somehow, some way and we're going to stop him. That's the first step," Bonnie said.

Fargo's eyes hardened on the two young women. "You told me a bald-faced lie and it seems you're as quick to accuse without proof as you are to shoot. That doesn't cut it with me, so I'll be moving on."

"To bring Horace Gregory his mail route."

"To do the job I was hired to do," Fargo said.

"And forget about right and wrong," Mary said with a sneer. "We thought someone riding an Ovaro like that might have some feelings for horses. Our mistake."

He swore at their disdainful righteousness as he wheeled the Ovaro in a tight circle. "I've feelings about being lied to," he said and set off at a fast canter. He didn't look back but felt their eyes as he rode away. They still held that air of bruised angels in tattered armor. They were carrying their own banner, right or wrong, and wouldn't be dissuaded by anything so simple as reason. But they instinctively knew where to strike, he grunted, as he thought about Mary's remark.

But they were also perfectly willing to lie and to ignore

the law to pursue their convictions. But wasn't that always the way with those convinced of their own righteous causes? He just couldn't swallow all their accusations, made of snippets and half-formed pieces, none with the substance of proof. The hell with them. He had a job to do. He sent the Ovaro up a slope and started west.

4

Fargo had almost reached the crest of a narrow ridge when he spied the row of bronze-skinned figures on their short-legged Indian ponies. He halted and faded back into the trees as the Indians moved downward and took a path that led away from him. He squinted and peered at the markings on a wrist gauntlet one of the braves wore. Pawnee, he grunted as he followed the squared design of the beadwork. He counted eight half-naked riders. He let them disappear from sight, waited a few minutes longer and then nosed the pinto from the trees and continued his way to the top of the ridge.

He rode along a deer trail he had decided would be an ideal place to begin, when he suddenly reined to a halt. The line of Pawnee stayed in his mind. They were moving toward the hollow. Maybe they'd switch direction. Then maybe they wouldn't. "Damn," Fargo swore as he spun the pinto around and started down the slope. He put the horse into a gallop when he reached the flat land and kept the pace over two small hills. When he reached the line of box elder that bordered the hollow of land he heard shots, sporadic rifle fire punctuating a steady chorus of war whoops and high-pitched cries. He hurried through the trees, reached the other end of them and yanked the rifle from its saddle case as he reined to a halt and leaped from the horse.

The war whoops came from trees facing the house and along two sides. He crouched as he watched three arrows sail through the air to lodge into one side of the house. Two bronze-skinned figures rose, ran on open ground for a moment and two shots came from the house. Both were well wide of their mark. Another pair of arrows came from the brush and landed in the ground a few feet from the door of the house. Fargo saw other arrows littering the ground and a few more imbedded into the house. Another Pawnee ran from the brush and two more shots came from the house, again both way off the mark. The Keegan girls were shooting damn poorly, he observed. Not at all like the kind of marksmanship he had seen them exhibit. Maybe they were nervous, frightened. He'd seen Indian attacks unnerve others.

The Pawnee had them trapped inside the house, though they were making no effort to rush it. They seemed strangely content with wild shouting and wilder volleys of arrows. Fargo raised the rifle to his shoulder. It was time to let the Pawnee know that their victims were not alone. That was often enough to send Indians running. In general, the Indian disliked the unknown—disliked being uncertain who or how many he was up against. And being ambushed was an especially bad mark around the council campfires. Suddenly, a Pawnee emerged from one side of the brush and ran toward the side of the house, tomahawk in hand. He seemed to be heading for one of the windows when he swerved toward the front. Fargo, the rifle to his shoulder, fired just as the Pawnee hurled the tomahawk into the wooden boards of the house inches from the corner.

The heavy rifle slug slammed into the Indian and his figure went into a twisting half somersault as he fell sideways and collapsed in front of the house. The wild, whooping cries broke off, the arrows stopped sailing through the air and the girls stopped shooting. An abrupt silence fell over the scene. Then three Pawnee rushed from the brush and Fargo raised the rifle again. But they ran straight for the still form on the ground. Fargo saw the door of the house open and Bonnie come out, the rifle hanging from her hand. She stood quietly and watched as the Pawnee picked up the dead buck and hurried into the trees with him. In moments, Fargo heard the Indian ponies pushing their way through the trees and he stepped forward and walked toward Bonnie as Mary came from the house.

"*You*!" Bonnie exploded. "Shit, you killed him."

"Damn right. He was charging the house," Fargo said.

"He was just going to put an axe into the wall," Bonnie said.

Fargo frowned at the two young women. "What the hell are you talking about?"

"They do this once very few months. They make a lot of noise, fire arrows into the place and end with sticking a tomahawk into the wall. But they don't try to hurt us. They shoot around us and we shoot around them. It's their way of telling us the hills are still theirs and we tell them we intend staying. It's a ritual—their ritual with us," Mary said. "Nobody ever gets hurt."

"And now you've gone and fucked it up, damn you," Bonnie flung at him. "You've wrecked it. You killed one of them."

"Now, hold on a damn minute," Fargo said, his own anger rising. "How the hell was I supposed to know you had this crazy relationship going? I came back to stop an attack, which I was afraid I'd find, and to save your damn necks."

"He's right there," Mary said to Bonnie, a grim weariness in her voice. "He'd no way of knowing anything but what he saw."

Bonnie glowered at Fargo. "He could've waited and watched a few minutes longer. Then he'd have seen something was different," she insisted. Fargo said nothing but remembered wondering why their marksmanship was so uncharacteristically poor. Maybe he could have waited a few moments longer, but he refused to take the blame for what had been a normal reaction. And an attempt to save their lives.

"You two are bad news. Lies, wild accusations, half-cocked causes. Everything that involves you is somehow bent out of shape and off center," he said.

"Too damn bad," Bonnie shot back.

"And you've not got common decency. I came back to save your necks and you can't even say thanks," he said.

"All you did was put our necks God knows where and I don't feel much like saying thanks for that," Bonnie returned.

Fargo's eyes were hard as he peered at her. She was a hardnosed little bitch, probably the harder of the two. "Go to hell, honey," he said and turned away. Then Mary's voice came.

"I'll thank you for trying," she said. "You get an 'A' for effort. But Bonnie's got a point. We don't know where we stand with them, now."

Fargo shrugged and knew he had no answer. He gave a low whistle and the Ovaro came out of the trees to halt beside him. "Maybe you two ought to think about getting out of here for a while," he said.

"Horace Gregory would like that," Bonnie snapped.

Fargo turned to mount the pinto when he saw the line of box elder rustle, the low branches moving. The Colt was in his hand as he backed toward Mary and Bonnie and he saw the figures emerge from the trees—at least ten, now. Bonnie and Mary raised their rifles as they backed toward the house and Fargo moved with them, his eyes on the tall, well-muscled Pawnee that stepped out from the others. The Indian had long black hair, heavy with bear grease, a strong face with the semiflat Pawnee nose. He wore only a breech-clout and carried a tomahawk in the rawhide waistband.

He lifted one arm and pointed at Fargo with cold imperiousness. Pawnees spoke the Caddoan language, along with the Wichita and the Arikara. But this Indian spoke in a guttural Crow and Fargo allowed a grim smile. The Pawnee knew that Crow was the language most white men knew, really a branch of the Siouan. "He wants me in exchange for the dead tribesman," Fargo said.

"Or else?" Mary asked.

"They attack for real," Fargo said.

"Can we hold out?" Mary said.

He spoke over his shoulder without turning, his eyes on the Indian. "I don't know. Not long, I'd guess and not at all if they use fire arrows," he said and let thoughts race through his head. "I could hit the saddle and run for it, draw some of them off while you get to the stable and make your own run," he said.

"We'd have to saddle up. They'd have us," Mary said.

"Too bad," he heard Bonnie say and felt the rifle pushed into the small of his back. "Drop your guns, Fargo. The rifle, then the Colt," Bonnie's voice said and he turned to stare at her.

"You're kidding," he said.

"Do I look like I'm kidding?" she asked and he peered at the unsmiling seriousness of her face. "Sorry," she said. "Drop the guns."

He let the rifle fall from his hand and then dropped the Colt beside it. "You little bitch," he said to Bonnie.

"Some things just decide themselves," she said.

"If you have no guts and no principles," he growled.

"It's the most basic human emotion. It's called survival," Bonnie said.

"It's called real neat. You get off the hook by giving me to them, and Horace Gregory doesn't get his mail route," Fargo said.

"It just happens to work out," Bonnie said.

"Bullshit," Fargo rasped and glanced at Mary. She shrugged and had the grace to look unhappy. "Thanks," he tossed at her. She shrugged again and looked away.

Two more Pawnee came forward to bring their mounts alongside the Ovaro as Fargo climbed onto the horse. Another brave brought the tall Pawnee his pony. The Indian

55

climbed onto the mount with a grave nod at Bonnie and Mary. The other braves fell in behind and in front as Fargo was led from the hollow, through the trees and up a slope. He took in the tall Pawnee's stone-faced expression. They had made their weird accommodation with the two girls, but they were still Pawnee. There'd be no accommodation with him, he realized.

But he'd bide his time. He still had the thin, double-edged throwing knife in the calfskin holster around his leg. He'd have to wait for the right moment to use it. He'd only have one chance. He had to make it count. They were obviously taking him back to their camp to make a ceremony of him and Fargo's lips tightened at the thought. This was not a ceremony at which he wanted to be the guest of honor. His eyes went to the Pawnee leader again. He wore no chief's eagle feather. No chief's headdress hung from his mount. He was a war-party leader, a rank given to braves who had shown skill and courage that made him a special person, but not yet fit to sit in tribal councils. And now he'd take one more step forward in camp circles.

Fargo swore silently and his eyes moved across the terrain. They were still moving up a gentle slope, riding higher into the hills when he saw a wide passageway with heavy hackberry on both sides. They had just entered the passageway when the volley of shots exploded. He ducked instinctively, but saw two of the nearest braves topple from their mounts with red scrapes along their shoulders. He saw the Pawnee next to him try to whirl and fall as a shot grazed the side of his temple. The others were scattering, including the Pawnee leader. Fargo saw two more go down with shots that grazed their chests.

He laughed as he spun the Ovaro. The shots were all meant to graze, damn near perfect marksmanship, and coming from the hackberry trees at his left. He sent the Ovaro racing for the trees, completely certain who he'd find there. As he burst into the first line of the trees he saw Mary pulling up onto her mount, then Bonnie already in the saddle. "This way," Bonnie called and led the way down a narrow moose trail that cut through the center of the slope. He followed both girls as they came out into a narrow valley. They crossed it and then turned into another hollow, raced up a slope in the middle hills. Finally he saw the hollow where their house was.

"They'll be coming on our heels, you know," Fargo said as he leaped to the ground and Mary and Bonnie did the same.

"I know," Mary said. He found Bonnie crossing in front of him.

"Change of heart? Attack of conscience?" he slid at her as he scooped the Sharps and the Colt from the ground.

"Getting softheaded," she sniffed. Fargo didn't reply and his eyes narrowed as he heard horses crashing through the trees.

"Shouldn't we get inside?" Mary asked from near the door. Fargo's lips were a thin, tight line, his eyes on the trees. Nothing had happened to improve their chances and he pulled his lips back in distaste. By now the Pawnee leader had realized the shots of the ambush had deliberately avoided killing anyone. The girls had sent a message again. But that message wouldn't be enough to turn aside the Pawnee's need for vengeance. He'd still want his pound of flesh.

The Pawnee came through the trees, the tall, war-party leader a few paces in front of the others. Fargo knew he'd have to move boldly. He'd need the power of tradition and tribal honor, first, and then the power of his muscled body, every last bit of it. The Indian halted as Fargo strode up to him and motioned for him to dismount. The Pawnee cast a quick glance at Mary and Bonnie, who had stepped foward a few paces, and then swung from the horse. Fargo used sign language with a few words in Crow and watched the Indian's eyes bore into him. The others were watching, Fargo knew. In fact, he counted on their concentration. He motioned again, using sign language to repeat what he had said before to the Pawnee leader. He had challenged the man to single combat, a contest to prove who was the greater warrior. It was impossible for the Pawnee to turn him down, Fargo knew. To refuse the challenge would be against all tribal custom and tradition.

The Pawnee raised his arm and the others fell back. With a sweeping motion, the Indian drew his tomahawk and held it aloft. Fargo nodded his understanding of the gesture. The Pawnee wanted to use weapons. Fargo was aware he had little choice but to agree. The Indian had one of the others toss a tomahawk to Fargo's feet. Fargo leaned over and picked it up. They would both be armed, but that didn't make it a fair contest and the Pawnee knew it. The tomahawk was his weapon—a part of him—while it was simply an axe to the white man, awkward to the hand. The Indian began to circle and Fargo's eyes flicked to the man's feet. Fargo saw at once that the Pawnee moved well, his left foot stepping out first, carrying the weight of his body movements.

Fargo fixed the fact in his mind and returned his eyes to the Indian's hands as the man moved forward with a quick, darting thrust of the tomahawk. Fargo met the blow with his own weapon, aware that it was meant to draw him out. He was ready for the quicker blow that followed, an upward swing of the short axe. He ducked and parried and the Indian moved forward again, his left foot leading was he swung another blow. Fargo again parried it, but the quickness of the next blow took him off-guard—a vicious upswing. He felt the wind against his face from the tomahawk as he managed to twist away. He brought his own weapon around in a counterblow, a flat swing which the Indian easily avoided and countered with a fast, downward blow. Fargo ducked away, but just barely, and he cursed the brave's skill and speed.

He moved backward and the Indian came after him, tossing off two feints, one to the right, the other to the left. Fargo felt the tension in his body as he tried to be ready for the real blow. It came, from directly in front of him—a sudden charge as the tomahawk spun in a quick succession of up and down swings. Fargo flung himself sideways in a dive, rolled and got to his feet as the Pawnee charged again. But this time, the Indian swung the tomahawk in short, chopping blows from side to side. Fargo parried one, then another, and managed a third with his own weapon. But the fourth blow got through and he felt the glancing power of the axe against his shoulder.

He staggered, dropping to one knee as the Pawnee charged in swinging and the blow raked his hair. With the Indian almost on top of him, Fargo had room only to bring the broad side of the tomahawk up and smash it into the man's abdomen. The Pawnee grunted in pain, stepped back for a moment and Fargo brought his tomahawk around in an upward arc, as though he were delivering a right hook. But the Indian's reactions were both quick and smart. Most men would have tried to pull back and they'd have taken the full force of his follow-up blow, but the Pawnee dropped low, rolled forward and brought his own weapon up almost from the ground. Fargo felt the wave of pain wash over him as the tomahawk crashed into his ribs and he gave thanks that it was only the flat side of the weapon.

He staggered sideways, flung himself almost in a back flip and managed to avoid the Pawnee's next blow. He scrambled to his feet as the Indian missed with a wild swing, but saw the man come forward again. Fargo felt the sweat running down his face and realized he was breathing hard. The Pawnee was too adept with the tomahawk and Fargo felt his own axe still clumsy in his hand. The Indian moved toward him and Fargo backed and circled. He tried a feint, but the Pawnee's weapon was raised in an instant parry. Fargo tried two more swinging blows and they were avoided or parried. He had to twist away from counterblows that were becoming increasingly closer. He suddenly realized that the tomahawk was doing him more harm than good. He was simply not practiced enough with it. His every blow exposed him to a counterblow that came perilously close. The weapon was asking him to make moves he simply couldn't make.

He took a step backward, went into a half crouch as his foe came forward again. Knowing it was more a gesture than anything else as far as he was concerned, he sent the tomahawk hurtling through the air at the Pawnee. The man took a split second to recover from his surprise and then easily avoided the axe. Fargo saw him smile as he took the act to be one of desperation. *Not yet, sonny,* Fargo muttered silently and let the Indian come at him. He felt freed, lighter and looser. This time he weaved as the Pawnee swung, dropped low and came up instantly as the tomahawk whizzed over his head. He smashed a winging left hook into the Indian's jaw and the man staggered backward, twisting away. Fargo pulled back the right cross he was about to throw.

He let the brave come at him again. Fargo waited for split seconds as the Pawnee leaped forward with a swipe of his weapon. Then Fargo twisted as he ducked and sank a hard right into his foe's ribs as the force of the leap carried the Indian past him. The man grunted, sprang back. Fargo moved closer to him and saw the anticipation forming in the Pawnee's burning black eyes. The Indian tensed, his tomahawk half-raised, ready to strike down and Fargo paused, waiting. The Pawnee moved first. His left foot leading, he started forward, raising his weapon. Fargo brought his own foot down with all his weight on the Indian's left foot. The man cried out in pain and the blow from the tomahawk went sideways. His foot still atop the Pawnee's moccasined extremity, Fargo threw a whistling uppercut with all the strength of his muscled shoulders behind it.

The blow smashed into the Indian's jaw and the man staggered backward, trying not to fall. Fargo's left hook landed right on the point of his jaw and the Pawnee dropped flat on his back and the tomahawk fell from his hand. Fargo scooped the weapon up as the Pawnee shook his head to clear his eyes. Dropping down over the Indian, Fargo brought the tomahawk down in a pile-driver blow that would have split the man's head in two. But he stopped the blade a fraction of an inch from the Indian's forehead and saw the terror in the man's eyes as he thought death was upon him. Fargo held the blade there for a long moment and then pushed to his feet. The Pawnee rose onto his elbows, his breath coming back in a deep sigh of relief.

Fargo tossed the tomahawk on the ground and walked away. The gesture had been made. The Pawnee knew its meaning. All of the Indians knew. He had won and spared his foe's life. But there was a price. That, too, was understood all around.

He watched the Indian pull himself onto his pony. He rode slowly into the trees and the others followed.

Fargo turned to Mary and Bonnie Keegan. "They won't be back, not even to play games anymore," he said. "There are codes. They'll abide by them."

"Thank you," Mary said, and Fargo nodded and realized the dusk was moving quickly over the hills.

"Thanks for coming after me," Fargo said. "Whatever decided you to." He cast a glance at Bonnie. Her face was set.

"Of course, it won't stop you from going on for Horace Gregory," she sniffed.

"No, it won't," Fargo said. "This was separate. You keep trying to connect things that don't connect."

"That depends on how you see things," Bonnie disagreed and strode into the house. Her high, round breasts bounced as she stomped across the ground. Fargo returned his eyes to Mary as the last of the light faded.

"Bonnie believes everything connects," Mary said with a small smile. "Night's come down. You can't break trails in the dark. We've extra room. A last night in a bed before the trail?"

"It's tempting, but I don't think Bonnie will welcome the idea," Fargo said.

"I know Bonnie. All this has upset her and when she's upset she goes into one of her dark moods. She's having a drink right now inside. She'll have three more and pass out," Mary said. "I'll toss in leftover stew," she added and he shrugged and followed her into the house.

Bonnie was in the kitchen, at the table with a bottle of rye and a shot glass in front of her. She fastened Fargo with a glower. "I offered him a bed for the night," Mary said.

"Figured you would," Bonnie said.

"No need for me to stay if it bothers you that much," Fargo said.

"Doesn't bother me. Failing bothers me. Horace Gregory winning out bothers me. Beautiful horses being slaughtered bothers me," she said and poured another whiskey for herself. He felt a surge of sympathy for her. She held fiercely to an inner integrity, twisted as it might be.

He went outside to unsaddle the Ovaro and when he returned, Mary had the stew ready. He sat down at the table. Bonnie had only a few mouthfuls, finished the whiskey and left without a word to anyone, closing the door to an adjoining room behind her. He saw Mary's tiny shrug.

"She often get like this?" Fargo asked.

"Only when she's real down," Mary said.

"You never get that down, I take it," Fargo said.

"I'm better at hoping," she said.

He helped her clear the dishes. She moved with quiet grace, the slightly shallow breasts curving upwards at the bottom in a pleasing line. When the dishes were cleaned and put back on a shelf, she showed him to a small room at the other side of the house, neat and clean with a double bed and a small lamp. She turned the lamp on low and paused in the doorway. "You'll be leaving early, I'd guess," she said.

"Before you're awake," he told her and she nodded once and closed the door. He undressed and stretched out across the bed, pulling a sheet across his groin as the night had stayed warm. The day retold itself in his thoughts. He had blundered, unwittingly, and the always close-to-the-surface passions of the untamed land were quick to explode. But he'd been able to salvage a kind of victory out of the spectre of disaster. Skill, strength, luck—they'd all played a part. But nothing else had changed. The Keegan cousins were still consumed with their mission, still willing to lie and cast accusations without proof. And he still had a job to do. He'd leave them to their causes, justified or otherwise, and their phantom rustlers.

The lamp gave a dim light and he started to reach over to turn it out when he heard the doorknob turn. His hand was on the Colt on the floor alongside the bed when Mary stepped into the room. She wore a gray cotton nightdress, almost floor-length. He took his hand from the Colt and lay back as she came toward the bed. "Couldn't sleep," she said.

"Bothered by having a man in the house?" He smiled.

"Not by itself," she said, but he saw her eyes slowly move up and down his smoothly muscled body. "But Bonnie was right. You are one fine-looking sample, I must say," she murmured.

"Make believe I bowed," Fargo said.

She brought her eyes back to his face. "I kept thinking how you put your life on the line for us," she said. "You could have run for it alone and probably made it."

"Maybe," he allowed.

"I'm thinking that calls for something more than just words," Mary Keegan said, taking a step closer to the bed.

"Are you really thinking that?" Fargo asked.

A faint smile touched the edges of her lips. "It's a good excuse, isn't it?" She half shrugged.

"Good as any I've heard," he agreed. With a sudden,

quick motion, Mary lifted the nightgown and pulled it up over her head and flung it aside to stand before him absolutely naked. His eyes took in her broad shoulders, her surprisingly pale skin and her breasts sweeping down in a long curve to cups that were full enough. Each was topped by a very red nipple and almost as red areola. A narrow waist moved down to a flat abdomen and he paused for a moment at a very curly, very black triangle that pointed to the meeting place of smooth-fleshed thighs—a little on the thin side but nonetheless shapely enough. His eyes swept her again. She had a body in which no single feature took one's breath away and yet all together held an unassuming appeal.

She came down to him, her knees onto the bed, her arms reaching and he gathered her to him. She was tight against him at once, her body not as muscled as he'd expected. He rolled onto his side with her and his hands cupped one of the longish breasts. Mary Keegan gave a tiny cry of pleasure. Very soft breasts to the touch, even the cups were malleable. Mary Keegan cried out softly as he let his thumb rub gently back and forth over the very red nipple. Her hands pressed into his chest as her mouth opened, and drew him in—wet wanting, lips quivering, tongue seeking. Her kisses were fervent, edging wildness and then, abruptly, she pulled back and he saw her brown eyes peering hard at him, studying his face, appraising and searching. Then, just as abruptly, her mouth was on his again, all the fervor returned.

He moved his lips down the side of her neck, skittered a soft path across her collar bone and down over one long-curved breast, licking the soft shallowness of it until he reached the cup. He drew the very soft mound into his mouth, pulled gently. His tongue circled the red nipple and Mary Keegan screamed softly. Her lean body twisted from one side to the other, hips and legs held together all moving as one, a sensuous motion, at once pristine and provocative. His hand moved down, slowly caressing the flat abdomen, pausing to circle the tiny indentation and then slide down over the very curly black triangle. "Oh, oh my God," Mary breathed as his hand moved through the soft wiry nap, pressed down over the pubic mound that seemed to have risen. Even there the touch of her was soft and pliable and his hand slid further, down to where her thighs, still held tightly together, formed a closed "V."

He pressed gently with the tip of one finger, then with his hand—delicate prodding, gentle pressure. He pushed into the soft flesh of her inner thighs as, with his other hand, he cupped one breast. His finger curled into the dark spot at the end of the curly triangle. He felt the moistness and suddenly, with a cry that burst from her, Mary's thighs fell open and she arched her hips upwards, fell back and arched again. "God, oh, God, yes, yes . . . ah, ah . . . Jesus," she moaned as her pelvis kept moving up and down, thrusting, imploring. He cupped his hand around the flowing moistness of her and she screamed at his touch and he heard a wild laughter of consummate pleasure in her voice. He touched, probed deeper and she was flowing, all welcoming, all wanting and he felt her thighs rubbing against his legs, lifting to all but circle his buttocks.

"Take me, dammit, take me, quick, quick," Mary Keegan breathed, a sudden desperation in her voice. "I'm going to come, oh, God, oh God." He felt his own response to her excitement, her urgent wanting enveloping, pulling him along with it and he came over her, thrust forward and felt her warmth close around him, pathway smoothed with her deliquescent welcome. "Aiiiiieeee!" Mary cried out, a half scream riding on gasped breath, and she was pumping furiously, her body moving with only the senses in control. He saw her short, brown hair flip up and down as every part of her quivered and bucked. Her thighs came up high, locked around his hips. Suddenly Mary Keegan almost flung herself from the bed, heels dug in, pelvis arched, carrying him up with her. Her arms locked around his neck as she screamed, over and over—short, high, staccato screams—and he felt the pulsations of her climax flow around him and he heard his own groan as he was swept along with her.

Her screams ended but her pulsing softness continued as he stayed with her and her voice was suddenly almost weak. "Oh, my God, oh, my God, oh, yes, oh yes . . . good God yes," she whispered in a soft breathlessness. She was still pulsing around him as he sank down on the bed with her and his mouth found one of the softly pliant breasts. Her arms circled his neck, held him there and still she pulsed, inside surges of the senses, the body unwilling to accept the ebbing of ecstasy. But finally she lay with him, her breath coming in long, slow draughts. His eyes took in the long, slightly concave curve of her breasts, the supple softness of her and the quiet, unassuming appealingness of her body. Like Bellwort, she was, he thought, with the same modest, under-stated loveliness.

She turned, pushed onto one elbow and shook her short, dark brown hair and her eyes stayed on him. "God, you're something special," she crooned.

"You weren't exactly Miss Reluctant," he said.

"Never been that way with anyone before," Mary Keegan murmured. "Surprised myself."

"Maybe too long between drinks," Fargo offered.

"That'd be too easy an answer," she said. "I think you bring out the best in a woman. Or the worst." He laughed and she pressed the very soft breasts into his face and settled down against him with a deep sigh. She pushed herself away after a few moments and swung from the bed. "I'll let you get some sleep, now," she said, pulling the nightgown over herself and he watched her walk to the door. She paused, looked back at him. "You see, no connections," she said.

"The way it ought to be," he nodded and she closed the door after her. He lay back, turned off the lamp and the room was instant blackness. They each had their own strange integrity, he decided, closed his eyes and let sleep sweep over him.

He woke with the first rays of the new sun. He washed with the water in a large porcelain basin atop the dresser and pulled on his clothes. He tiptoed from the house and quickly saddled the Ovaro. When he finished, he started to lead the horse away from the house when the figure stepped from behind the well, the early sun glinting on long, light-brown hair. She wore a gray skirt and no blouse but the top of her slip was cut high enough to at least bow to modesty. Her high, very round breasts pushed at the beige silk, drawing it tight, but he saw only smooth contours and not even the hint of a tiny point. Her round shoulders thrust back, she moved toward him.

"Expected you'd be leaving with the dawn," Bonnie Keegan said. "I wanted to say I'm sorry for being so rotten last night."

"Consider it said," he said. He held his hand out to her.

"I'm not much for shaking hands," she said and he found her lips against his, soft fullness, lingering for but a moment and then she stepped back, a half-smile touching her lips now. "I know, Mary says I've a bold way with men." Bonnie shrugged. "I wish I could get her to loosen up a little."

"Keep working on it," Fargo said and climbed onto the horse.

"No hard feelings," Bonnie said. "We all do what we have to do."

"That's right," Fargo said. "Good luck to you." He put the pinto into a slow trot and glanced back to see her return to the house, the sun on her round, bare shoulders. He sent the horse through a break in the trees and up a slope. There'd been too many delays. He had a lot of time to make up. The thick foliage of the hills beckoned him as he crested a ridge and rode northward. A moose trail appeared and he headed toward it. He halted at the start of it where a twisted cottonwood rose up, its outline unmistakable. He drew the notepad from his pocket and began his markings. The task was under way at last.

5

By the day's end, he was pleased. He'd made better progress than he'd expected. Moose and deer trails interconnected and often led him to narrow ravines. There were some sharp turns, but for the most part the route he was blazing led through the center of the hills. When he camped for the night alongside a cluster of shadbush, his notepad held not only trail lines but a number of guide marks. The twisted cottonwood came first, marking the start of the trail, then a pointed rock of gray granite, some twenty feet high. After that, a bent and gnarled bur oak that marked a sharp turn in the route and finally, a pair of tall cedars that grew side by side, trunks touching each other.

He put the notepad away, undressed and stretched out on his bedroll and the warm night quickly brought sleep. He was in the saddle soon after the morning sun turned the hills a soft gold and he followed a path that ran straight for almost two miles. He could see the terrain on all sides as he rode and he spied herds of wild horses, some running together, others grazing. And he saw deer, moose and elk. A big grizzly high up in the hills stood up for a moment and then disappeared into the brush. Suddenly he found himself realizing that the trail he blazed certainly let its rider take in everything. A man riding his trail would see every herd of horses, every herd of deer, every lone rider and every band of horsemen that moved through the center of the hills.

Mary and Bonnie's words intruded in his thoughts, perhaps

no more true or substantive but relevant. He pushed them aside and sent the pinto forward in a canter. The trail sloped upward and he halted to mark his notepad. He'd gone perhaps another quarter of a mile when he saw the land to his left flatten out and, slightly below where he rode, a ranch came into view. It was a good-sized spread. He counted three corrals besides the main house, stables and bunkhouse. He swung from the trail and rode down to the ranch where cowhands were working with nearly fifty horses spread out in the three corrals. He saw the sign over a wooden arch that served as a symbolic more thn an actual gate:

WILL STEDMAN'S
FINE HORSES

He rode under the arch and approached the house, a long, low structure, typical of ranch houses on the prairie. He was still taking in the building when a man emerged, grayish hair cut short, an amiable, open face with gray eyes that were shrewdly appraising. Fargo saw the man's eyes linger on the Ovaro and a smile edged his lips. "You must be Will Stedman," he said.

The man glanced at him with mild surprise. "That's right but I'm not wearing my name anywhere," he said.

"Yes, you are," Fargo said. "In your eyes. In the way you looked at my Ovaro."

Will Stedman laughed, a deep chuckle, as Fargo swung from the saddle. "One for you, mister," the man said.

"The name's Fargo—Skye Fargo. I'm marking a trail through these hills for Horace Gregory's mail route. I thought I'd stop by to ask you some questions if you don't mind."

"No, go ahead. I heard Gregory applied for a mail route," Stedman said.

"You have any trouble with that?" Fargo questioned, his eyes sharp on the man.

Will Stedman's lips pursed thoughtfully. "No, can't say that I do," he answered.

"You're not bothered by the fact that the Butterfield Overland Despatch and the Pike's Peak Express run on both sides of these hills?" Fargo questioned.

Will Stedman returned a broad smile. "You've been talking to the Keegan cousins," he said.

It was Fargo's turn to smile. " 'Fraid so," he admitted. "Seems you don't have their concern about rustlers."

"I do. I've had horses rustled. It's not just horses being rustled that had the Keegan girls up in arms," Will Stedman said.

"And how come they don't bother you rounding up wild horses?" Fargo asked.

"As I said, it's not rounding up mustangs that bothers them. It's what's done with the horses. I saddle-break the horses I round up, drive them to Kansas City where I sell them to the buyers from eastern riding schools," Stedman explained.

"You believe what the Keegan girls say about Horace Gregory?" Fargo asked.

Stedman wrinkled his face. "I've nothing to make me believe them but I've no respect for anyone who deals with Robert Rossand. Rossand's no good, a thief, a swindler and, I'm told, a murderer. Yet he has connections in high places in Washington. No local lawman anywhere has been able to jail him. All I know is that Horace Gregory deals with him, but I don't know for what or how."

"Which means they could be way off on their ideas about him," Fargo said.

"Yep. Or they could be right," Will Stedman said.

Fargo grimaced at answers that left him in exactly the same place. "Thanks for your time," he told Will Stedman. "Maybe I'll drop by again."

"Anytime," Stedman said and Fargo left with a long

glance at the horses being worked with in the corrals. Perhaps twenty more than he had first estimated, he decided as he headed back into the passage that ran down the center of the hills.

The trail turned higher, led to a ridge and he saw it break in two. He explored both and chose the one that ran along the ridge. He marked the chosen spot in his notepad: two fallen tree trunks that lay half-atop each other. The path he explored stayed wide enough even as it curved back and forth, yet kept mainly to the center of the hills. Finally he drew to a halt and found a spot to bed down as night descended.

His meeting with Will Stedman stayed with him before he dropped off to sleep, not unlike a touch of dyspepsia. He realized he'd been looking for a way to completely dismiss Mary and Bonnie. But he hadn't been able to do it and he decided there was no point in pursuing it further. They'd remain an enigma and he went to sleep wanting only to be finished with the job and on his way.

That much of his wish came closer by the end of the next day as the rugged hill country began to dip sharply downward and he finally found himself peering across an expanse of relatively flat land with plenty of open space between tree cover. This was the end of the high country and Gregory had told him there was no need to go farther. He turned the Ovaro around and began to make his way back along the trail he had just marked.

When night came, he bedded down on the trail and was back in the saddle with the morning sun. He slowed when he passed Will Stedman's place, below and to his right now. He saw that some of the horses were being worked outside the corrals and another fifteen or so were tame enough to graze outside on their own. He rode on, his eyes sweeping the low valley that stretched east from Stedman's place and almost paralleled the trail he'd marked out.

He had another night to spend on the trail before he reached

72

Horace Gregory's place in the late afternoon of the next day. Gregory was playing with a half dozen of the dogs outside the compound when Fargo rode up. The man rose at once and came forward as a ranch hand herded the dogs back into the wire fence area.

"Done?" Gregory asked, his gravelly voice colored with anticipation.

"Done," Fargo said, dismounting.

"Let's go inside. This calls for a drink," Horace Gregory said and Fargo followed him into the house. One of the dogs Gregory had called a Bernese mountain dog lay on the floor and seemed entirely detached from anything going on around him. Gregory poured Fargo a bourbon and Fargo handed him the notepad. The man sat down with it at once, scanning the map and the markings Fargo had set down. "This is great. Perfect. Clear enough for a six-year-old to follow," Gregory said. He went to a wall safe and brought out the balance of the money still owed and pressed it into Fargo's hands. "Fine work, Fargo. You're every bit as good as I've heard," the man said. "You'll be going on now, I suppose."

"Soon. I might relax some in Hillsdale," Fargo said, finishing the bourbon in his glass.

Gregory walked outside with him to where day had begun to give way to the grayness of dusk. Fargo climbed onto the Ovaro, rode slowly from the ranch and glanced back to see Gregory playing with the big Bernese mountain dog. Fargo rode on and turned up a slope as he swore silently. He ought to be feeling differently than he did. He always felt satisfied after a job was done, large or small. But somehow this time satisfaction held itself back and he found himself riding through the darkness toward the house in the mountain hollow.

The lights burned brightly inside the house as he walked the Ovaro toward the front door. He had almost reached it, when he saw the lights go out and head the door open. One of the two poked a rifle through the open door, he was certain, though he couldn't really see. Maybe both of them, he thought. "Hold your fire, ladies," he called out and waited. The lamps were turned on and he saw Mary in the doorway lower her rifle.

"Didn't expect company," she said. "Sure as hell not you." Bonnie came from the house to stand next to her, both regarding him with flat stares.

"Thought I'd look in on you," Fargo said.

"We don't need looking after," Bonnie said darkly.

"Didn't say you did. Don't be so damn thorny," he tossed back at her and she uttered a tiny snort.

"You finish your trail making?" Mary asked.

"I did," he said.

"Then you'll be moving on," she remarked.

"I might relax some in Hillsdale, if they've an inn," he said and let his eyes send a silent message to Mary. She blinked back at him.

"Most men relax at Abe McAdoo's dance hall," Bonnie said and gave him a sidelong glance. "Though I can't see you as much for working girls. But then one can never tell."

"I'm not. Besides, the kind of relaxing I want is rest in a real bed and enjoying some good bourbon slowly," Fargo said.

"You turn in your trail to Horace Gregory yet?" Bonnie questioned, sharpness coming into her voice. He nodded and saw the fury flare in her eyes. "Then you can hightail it out of here," she snapped.

"Can't you two back off? At least till you've more than wild talk and unproven accusations?" Fargo exploded.

"We've enough to satisfy us. We'll be taking it further in our way and in our time," Bonnie said.

"And maybe get your heads blown off doing things you've no right to do," he said.

"We told you, there's right and there's right," Mary said.

"Get out of here, Fargo." Bonnie glowered. He looked at Mary and he knew she read his eyes as they reminded her of her visit to him. He hoped there'd be a softening in her that would give him more chance to reach them both with reason. He saw her eyes respond for a moment and then she looked away. She hadn't forgotten that night, she told him silently. It just wasn't enough to change things, especially not with Bonnie's adamant anger reaching out to hold her.

He felt his own anger rush forward. "You're beyond talking to, the both of you," he bit out and received only silence, Bonnie's made of stone, Mary's from uncomfortableness. Yet the result was the same.

He wheeled the pinto around and took off in a fast canter. He kept the horse at it as he climbed a fairly open slope under the moon's pale light. He slowed when he turned into a ridge that led eastward, but he was still muttering to himself. To hell with them both. He couldn't abide people who refused to even listen to reason. That certainly described Mary and Bonnie Keegan. Maybe they'd draw back some if they got to know Horace Gregory better. They'd see a man who enjoyed raising purebred dogs and was clearly fond of his animals. That didn't fit the picture of a man who'd round up mustangs to be slaughtered.

Only one thing was clear, Fargo grunted. He'd never felt so damn dissatisfied after finishing a job. He wanted to lay the blame for that on Mary and Bonnie Keegan but he knew that was a half-truth at best. He had seen the herd of horses race off by themselves—maybe spooked and maybe not—the entire incident seemed strange. And there were two perfectly good express mail routes on either side of the hills. Lastly, someone had been about to shoot Mary Keegan when he intervened. All strange, dark undercurrents that clung, refusing dismissal. Was he being foolish, following his inner feelings? He'd accused the girls of that when he full well knew the power of inside voices.

Maybe some relaxation would dispel it all and he could go his way with inner peace, he told himself as the buildings of Hillsdale came into sight—a dark cluster of shapes. It was late and the town was still. Only the dance hall sent a yellow finger of light into the street. But Fargo rode by to rein up in front of a small grayish-white structure where a worn sign over the doorway proclaimed bed and board. Inside, Fargo woke a baldheaded man asleep at a desk. "Room. Ground floor," Fargo said. "Couple of days, maybe."

The man handed him a room key and Fargo left to wake someone else, this time the stable boy at the town stables where he secured a roomy corner stall for the Ovaro. When he returned to the inn, he shed clothes and fell across the bed to sleep almost at once. He let himself sleep far later into the morning than he usually did and when he emerged from the inn, the town was a bustling place. He took in Owensboro Huckster wagons with their drop end-gates and Studebaker farm wagons and more than a few berry wagons carrying produce and plenty of pack mules with mining gear strapped onto their backs. Most of their owners either came from or were headed for the country around Pike's Peak, he was certain. The sharp, thickly grown hill country he had ridden through wasn't mining land.

He sauntered to the stable where he paid the day man for water and a hose and proceeded to clean and groom the Ovaro until the horse's coat fairly gleamed in the afternoon sun. He used his own stable rubber for a final polishing and finished with the hoof pick. It was an afternoon's work, and the night descended as he fed the horse with a bag of fresh oats. He walked back to the inn, had a tub drawn and washed, changed clothes and made his way up the now dark streets of Hillsdale to the dance hall.

His gaze traveled across the large room as he entered and he saw a a very open space on the floor and round tables taking up most of the rest of the room. The girls wore short skirts, black net stockings and filmy black tops. They were younger than most, he noted, only their eyes showing inner scars.

He eased himself into a chair at one of the tables and immediately found a young woman at his side. She was fairly tall, with dark hair, on the thin side with a face too young for such jaded eyes. "What's your pleasure, mister?" she asked.

"Some food and a drink, bourbon. No bar whiskey," Fargo said. "Roast chicken if you have it."

She nodded and offered a smile that once might have been seductive but was now simply mechanical. "And afterwards?"

"Depends on how I feel afterwards," Fargo said pleasantly and watched her walk away, the net stockings helping to give her legs more allure than they actually had. Another young woman, fuller busted and shorter, flashed him a smile as she passed, a little less mechanical but thoroughly commercial. His eyes traveled the dance hall as he relaxed. The customers were ordinary enough and he saw a few of them accompany girls up a rickety wooden staircase to the upper floor. There was no madam in the place, but before going upstairs each girl paused at a wiry figure standing at one end of the bar. The man wore a derby hat set rakishly on his head, a striped shirt with a red bow tie and a red garter around one arm. Dark, well-pressed trousers, completed his outfit. Fargo noted the gun stuck in the waistband of his belt—a Sharps four-barreled derringer, a small but deadly, fast-firing weapon.

The girl brought Fargo the bourbon and he took a taste. It wasn't bar whiskey but it wasn't terribly good bourbon either and he sipped it with the chicken when it came. He watched the man with the derby move around the room, a spring in his step. His wiry figure finally came to the table.

"Evenin', friend," he said pleasantly. "Haven't seen you in here before. I'm Abe McAdoo. This is my place," the man said without disguising the pride in his voice. "What brings you this way?"

Fargo smiled inwardly, took another sip of the bourbon. This was as good a time as any to get reactions. "Been visiting," he said. "Relatives of my aunt's, the Keegan girls." The inward smile almost became visible when he saw Abe McAdoo's face instantly redden.

"That's not a name anyone mentions in my place," the man said.

"You asked," Fargo said blandly.

"So I did," Abe McAdoo conceded unhappily.

"You had some problem with Mary and Bonnie Keegan?" Fargo asked innocently.

"Stinkin', rotten bitches, that's what they are. Damn near ruined my business. Came down here interfering, stirring up trouble," Abe McAdoo exploded.

"Someone tried to kill Mary Keegan about a week ago," Fargo remarked.

"More power to him," the man bit out, paused and fastened a glare at Fargo. "If you're thinking it was me, you're all wrong."

"Didn't think anything," Fargo said.

"Lots of folks around here haven't forgotten what they did," Abe McAdoo said. "Lots of folks don't want to see them around to try it again."

"What exactly did they do?" Fargo asked.

"Got my girls to walk out," the man said, lowering his voice and leaning closer. Fargo noted the girl that had waited on him and the shorter, fleshier girl nearby, were both listening. "They got my girls believing I wasn't splitting enough with them, treating them right, giving them time off on their own. Got them all riled up. And none of it any of their goddamn business. I had to close down for near a week."

"But you're in business now," Fargo said.

"And it costs every one of my customers more to get laid and more to get drunk. I tell you, a lot of folks have it in

78

for those two," Abe McAdoo said. He straightened up and drew his breath in. "Don't like to talk bad about a man's relatives but truth is truth."

"No matter to me. They're distant relatives," Fargo said and the man strolled away with a nod. On the thought that mediocre bourbon was better than no bourbon, Fargo ordered another as he sat back and watched the customers come and go. They seemed a pretty ordinary lot and he saw no one that appeared sullen or angry. But then, it was a highly casual survey, he realized, and maybe the angry ones came on other nights.

But Abe McAdoo had corroborated everything Horace Gregory had told him. Mary and Bonnie Keegan had interfered, made the girls another of their causes, rightly or wrongly. The fact bothered him and made him wonder if they simply took pleasure in stirring up trouble.

He finished the bourbon, paid and strolled out of the dance-hall with a nod to Abe McAdoo. Outside, he began to walk down the street toward the inn. He'd just reached the end of the dance hall when he saw a side door open and two young women hurried toward him. One was the girl who'd waited on him, the other one obviously her friend.

"Got a second, mister?" the taller one asked and he halted. "We heard Abe telling you about Mary and Bonnie. Well, they were right about everything. He didn't tell you that, of course."

"Maybe it wasn't any of their business but they were still right. He was treating us like shit and they made us see it and face up to him and we're a damn sight better off because of them," the other girl said.

"We just wanted you to know that, you being a relative and all," the taller one said.

"Much obliged, ladies," Fargo nodded and there was sincerity in the smiles they gave him before they hurried back through the side door.

Fargo walked on to the inn, undressed and stretched out

across the bed and found himself grimacing. Only a little while back he had wondered if the Keegan cousins simply took pleasure in stirring up trouble. The things the two dance hall girls had told him didn't erase that. But their words had added another disturbing note. Mary and Bonnie had been right, they'd said. Fargo frowned into the night. Were they right about Horace Gregory? They had no business stopping a man from rounding up wild horses, but were they right?

The question stuck inside him. He knew it would nag at him until he found out the truth of it. Once again he'd convinced himself to dismiss them and once again it became impossible. Damn, he swore silently and turned angrily onto his side. He'd let a night's sleep settle his churning thoughts down, he told himself and pulled slumber to him as though it were a blanket. He tossed and turned some, but finally dropped off to sleep and once again let himself enjoy the luxury of rising late. They were serving coffee in the small lobby of the inn and he had a cup, sipped it slowly and realized that the night's sleep had done nothing to clear up his mixed thoughts about Mary and Bonnie.

Some things just refused to resolve well, he reminded himself. Some things you just rode away from and left them to resolve themselves in their own way. He drained the coffee and walked down to the stable where he saddled the Ovaro and rode slowly from town and into the hills. He found himself moving toward the long valley where he had seen the herds of mustangs. And where he had watched phantom rustlers chase one herd into the night. He spied the dun-colored stallion again and watched a fair-size herd amble across the valley. Fine-looking animals, he muttered. No fancy show ring stock and no high hurdle jumpers but all good, sturdy riding stock. The idea of their being sent off for horsemeat stabbed at him and he felt his anger rise at the very thought.

But he'd no reason to believe that. He'd not been shown

the slightest proof, not even circumstantial evidence. Yet he had to wonder why a man would round up horses and not appear in the marketplace to sell them. Maybe he had enough individual buyers waiting to not need the horse auctions. Not very likely, yet not an impossibility. Thoughts kept leaping back and forth in his head, colliding with each other and he swore silently as he rode from the valley. He rode along some of the trail he had marked, saw another herd of mustangs below and finally turned and headed back to Hillsdale.

He'd take one more night of relaxation and then be on his way, he decided. Night had come over the town when he reached Hillsdale and he made his way to the dance hall for something to eat. That was a real enough reason, he told himself while aware that he had another one gnawing inside him. The tall, dark-haired girl saw him at once when he entered and came to the table as he sat down, her mechanical smile replaced by a cautious one. He had just ordered, when he heard the voice at his side and turned to see Abe McAdoo in what was plainly his uniform of derby and red bow tie.

"Didn't expect you'd be back, seeing as to what I said about the Keegan girls," the man remarked. "They being kin to you."

"Distant kin," Fargo said. "Besides, this is the only show in town." Abe McAdoo's smile was faintly smug as he walked away. Fargo ate leisurely, consumed two bourbons and watched the customers come and go. He'd just finished the second drink when the tall girl stopped at the table.

"There are other ways to relax," she said.

His lips pursed as he studied her for a moment. "Why not?" he said.

She looked uncomfortable for a moment as he rose to his feet. "Abe insists on money first. You pay me, I keep my part and give him the rest," she said.

He pressed the bills into her hand, waited as she went to the little wiry-figured man. Then she turned and beckoned to him with a glance. He met her at the stairs and she led him to a small but neat room on the second floor, a dim lamp with a red shade giving a softly suggestive glow.

Fargo sat down on the edge of the bed and the young woman started to undo the sheer top part of her outfit. "I'm Patty," she offered as she let the garment fall away and he took in long breasts, hanging flat with large nipples and absolutely nothing exciting about them. But then he wasn't in the mood to be excited, he reflected honestly and he reached a hand out to stop her as she started to undo her skirt.

"I want you to answer some questions for me, nothing else," he said and the girl frowned as he pulled her gently to the edge of the bed beside him.

"What if I can't answer them?" she asked.

He shrugged. "Your time's already paid for. My loss," he said.

"Never had this happen before," she muttered with the frown deepening.

"There's always a first time. I want you to put your thinking cap on," Fargo said. "Did you hear anybody actually say they were going to kill the Keegan girls?"

"A lot of the men said it, but it seemed they were just letting off steam," she answered.

"Did Abe McAdoo meet with anyone, a stranger come to town to see him?" Fargo queried.

"Not that I saw," she answered. "But he could have. I'm not here all the time and he could've met somebody outside or in back."

Fargo thought for a moment. "You know any of Horace Gregory's men?"

"Most of them stop in every so often," she nodded.

"You hear any of them talk about getting the Keegan girls?"

"No," she said.

"One last thing. Anybody come in during the past week or so with his forearm bandaged?"

She frowned in thought again. "No, not that I saw," she said and Fargo grimaced. She'd not been able to give him anything of help, except in an oblique way. If the man he'd stopped from shooting Mary Keegan had been a town regular, the chances were he'd have stopped in at the dance hall. It was also unlikely that if Horace Gregory had been behind it, he'd have used one of his own men. Which meant the would-be killer had been an outsider, a hired hand who'd surely taken off fast after having failed in his task. So he had more or less eliminated angry locals. That still left Gregory and Abe McAdoo. Fargo stood up.

"Thanks, Patty," he said.

She blinked. "We've time," she said.

"Maybe some other time," he smiled.

"Never been turned down before," she said with a pout forming on her young face.

"I'm not turning you down," he said and cupped her chin in his hand. She suddenly looked terribly lost and young and unhappy. "I'm turning myself down," he added, and she was quickly willing to accept his words. She slipped the top on and went downstairs with him.

"Abe's going to ask. What'll I tell him?" she said.

"Tell him you never saw anybody so fast in your life."

Fargo laughed and strode out of the dance hall. He led the pinto down the street to the stable, unsaddled the horse and returned to the inn. The baldheaded clerk motioned to him and handed him a folded square of notepaper. Fargo frowned down at the few words as he opened the sheet.

"You hire out for cash. Our cash is as good as Horace Gregory's. Consider yourself hired. We'll stop by in the morning."

Fargo grunted as he crumpled the note and tossed it into a nearby wastebasket. It was unsigned, but it didn't need a signature. They couldn't even write a note without their bristling, belligerent stamp on it. And their arrogant assumptions. He'd sure as hell not consider himself hired, he muttered. He'd decided to ride out come morning and leave it all behind him.

He swore softly. The damn note had ended that. Curiosity would make him stay long enough to hear them out. He made a wry smile as he went to his room and undressed. They knew that, of course, damn their cleverness. He stretched out on the bed and closed his eyes. One thought was firm in his mind before he went to sleep: They'd have to have something real to make him stay on.

6

Fargo had come back from the stable with the Ovaro and was waiting outside the inn when Mary and Bonnie Keegan rode to a halt and dismounted. Mary's light cotton blouse was snug against her breasts and he found himself remembering the long curve of them. Bonnie wore a plaid shirt that pulled tight and both wore riding britches. "You get our note?" Mary asked.

"Didn't think much of it," Fargo growled. "Say your piece."

"We want to hire you, cash down, whatever you want," Mary said.

"What for?" he asked.

"To nail Horace Gregory. We were right," Bonnie said.

"About what?"

"About Horace Gregory. Since you blazed that mail route for him, Will Stedman has had two herds rustled," Bonnie said, accusation in her tone.

Fargo thought for a moment. "Maybe it's pushing coincidence, but it doesn't mean Gregory's involved. Lots of people rustle horses," he said.

"We know that," Bonnie said impatiently. "But we know it's Gregory."

"No, you don't, dammit. You've hunches, conclusions, personal dislikes, but you don't know a damn thing," Fargo said.

"We want to hire you to get proof, catch him in the act," Mary said.

"Why me?"

"Because you got involved," Mary said.

"Not because I wanted to," Fargo protested.

"No matter." Mary shrugged. "And you saw one herd of mustangs take off all on their own. This is more of the same."

"More phantom rustlers?" Fargo frowned.

"That's right. Go talk to Will Stedman," Mary said.

"Cash hire, Fargo. Money is money," Bonnie tossed out.

"Shove it, sister," Fargo said and turned away.

"No, wait," Bonnie called out. "I take that back."

He halted, fastened her with a cold glare. "I thought you might take it if you saw it as just another job."

"Nothing's just another job," Fargo growled, and she offered apology with her eyes. "I'll talk to Stedman," he said.

"Does that mean you're hired?" Mary asked eagerly.

"Guess so," he muttered and saw their wide smiles.

"We've shopping to do here in town, but we'll be gone before you get back. Come to the house," Mary said.

"Don't wait up. I'll come visit when I've something to say," Fargo told them. They nodded in unison and rode away with waves of excited happiness flowing out from them.

Fargo climbed onto the pinto and rode from town in the other direction. He should have turned down the girls, he told himself, and gone on his way. But he had noticed something. The gnawing dissatisfaction inside him had somehow vanished. He grunted wryly and climbed a hillside and swung onto the route he had marked out. He stayed on it, again aware of how much of the land below it allowed a rider to see. He finally turned from it when he saw the buildings of the Stedman ranch appear. Will Stedman came out of the house as he rode up, his open face grim.

"You just happening by?" the man asked.

"Getting suspicious of everyone?" Fargo returned.

"That's right," Will Stedman said. " 'Specially somebody hired by Horace Gregory."

"You think Gregory's behind the rustling, too?" Fargo questioned with a moment's surprise.

"I don't know what I think," the man snapped back.

"Well, I did my job for Gregory. The Keegan girls have hired me to see what I can find out," Fargo said. "They're still talking about phantom rustlers."

"That's as good a name as any," Will Stedman said. "I've had men on watch every night, stationed one up on the west slope and another on the ridge. They couldn't miss seeing a band of rustlers approaching."

"But they didn't see them," Fargo said.

"Nobody and then suddenly a dozen of my horses are jumping and smashing their way out of the corral and running like hell through the ravine. By the time my men realized what was happening, they were out of sight."

"Your boys follow?"

Stedman grimaced. "No, they rode down looking for the rustlers, thought they'd find them in the trees back in the corral, maybe."

"But they didn't find anybody."

"Not a one. Same damn thing two nights later. I had sentries positioned up high enough to see any riders moving toward the place. There were no riders, but my stock bolted again and raced like hell down the ravine."

"Your boys follow this time?"

"No. By the time they came down off the hills and ridges, the herd was way gone. Truth is, just between us, I think they were afraid," Stedman said.

"Afraid?"

"Of following and being dry-gulched, one said, but I think it was more. I think they were afraid of what they couldn't see or understand. Maybe unnerved is a better word," Stedman said.

"Probably," Fargo agreed.

"Truth is, it is kind of scary. I mean, you just can't rustle a herd of horses without setting them off and that means riding into them shooting, shouting or cracking whips. There's no other way. You've got to get them running and keep them going," Stedman said.

"That's right," Fargo agreed. "I'll be stopping back, I'm sure. Meanwhile, keep your sentries out there. They may pick up something they've missed so far."

"Count on it. By the end of the week we'll be bringing in a new herd and I'll be moving the saddle-broke ones to the outside corral," Will Stedman said. "I sure hope you can get a handle on this real fast, Fargo."

"I'll be trying," Fargo said as he rode away. He took the trail again as he returned to the town. The low ravine from Stedman's spread ran southeast, he saw, toward Horace Gregory's place. The valley near Mary and Bonnie where he had seen the herd racing away also stretched in the direction of Horace Gregory's land. Perhaps just a coincidence. But perhaps not. He was still letting thoughts idle in his mind as night fell and he finally reached Hillsdale. When he halted at the stable, the stableboy was still there. He saw the boy watch him unsaddle the horse and lead the pinto into a corner stall.

"You're the one the Keegan girls hired," the boy remarked.

"How'd you know that?" Fargo frowned.

"I heard you rode a really fine-looking Ovaro," the boy said.

"You heard right. Give him a feedbag of oats," Fargo said.

"Yes, sir," the boy nodded and Fargo's frown stayed on his brow as he walked toward the dance hall.

When he entered, Patty saw him and came over to him at once as he sat down at a center table. He settled for a beef sandwich and a bourbon and the girl paused for a moment. "Heard Mary and Bonnie Keegan hired you," she said.

"Who told you that?" Fargo asked.

"Ben Still at the general store," the girl said and hurried away with his order. Fargo swore softly. Mary and Bonnie talked too much, he muttered. When Patty returned with his sandwich and the bourbon he was still frowning unhappily. He was halfway through his sandwich when he saw Abe McAdoo stroll toward him. The wiry-figured man halted at the table, his eyes appraising and with one hand he shifted his derby to an even more rakish angle.

"What makes a man let a couple of busybodies hire him?" McAdoo wondered aloud with an edge of disdain.

Fargo pushed down a flare of anger. "Same thing that makes a man run a whorehouse and call it a dance hall. Money," he said and watched McAdoo's eyes darken.

"I don't take kindly to that," McAdoo said.

"Your privilege," Fargo said between bites of his sandwich.

"I don't go around causing trouble," the man muttered.

"Me neither, 'less you're rustling horses," Fargo remarked.

"Just working for those two will mark you down with a lot of folks," McAdoo said threateningly.

"I'm real upset about that," Fargo said and the man walked away muttering to himself. Fargo finished the meal and left the dance hall to walk slowly back to the inn. He was still irritated at Mary and Bonnie for their loose tongues. He understood them, unfortunately. They felt smug, even triumphant. They enjoyed announcing they were no longer fighting alone. It was a kind of victory they had tossed at the town. But he still wished they had kept it to themselves, he grumbled as he went to his room, fell into bed and slept at once.

When he woke in the morning, he had no firm plans

formed. A little exploring was in order, he decided. He took the Ovaro and rode out to Horace Gregory's spread. He stayed in the thick hackberry near the rear of the ranch and saw some two dozen horses in the corrals. His eyes were narrowed as he watched two cowhands move among the horses. These were not mustangs, snorting and shying away from man. These horses stayed steady. They'd been worked with, broken to a saddle. Will Stedman's horses? He found himself wondering. He'd no way of knowing, not alone and he considered bringing Stedman back with him to look. His eyes went to the wire compound and saw Horace Gregory playing with the dogs, the swifter German shepherds running after sticks he threw, while the border collies and Bernese mountain dogs tugged on burlap sacks.

His eyes moved on to the front of Gregory's spread. Horses driven through the ravines or the valleys could easily be herded into Gregory's corrals. Again, no proof of anything by itself. He stayed in the trees as he saw Horace Gregory leave the compound and go to the stables. The man emerged soon after on a dark-brown gelding and three of his hands joined him as he rode from the ranch.

Fargo, staying in the tree cover, followed, cresting a slope as he kept Gregory in sight. The man took his hands up a hill, halted, and Fargo watched him gesture to the men, his arm movements not pointing to the clear gulley below but to the trees on either side of it. Fargo continued to peer out from the trees. Horace Gregory led his men along one line of trees, again motioning with his hands and then turning away to put his mount into a fast canter as he moved northeast.

Fargo hung back as he followed, but it was becoming more difficult as Gregory left the hills for open country. He was riding toward Hillsdale, Fargo realized suddenly and he reined to a halt in a cluster of bur oak. He let Gregory and his men disappear from view while he waited in the cool shade of the trees. He finally moved the pinto forward into the open. He followed the road toward town at a leisurely pace and had the Ovaro at a walk as he reached town and rode down Main Street. He was approaching the dance hall, when he saw Gregory come out, his three men at his heels. Fargo watched Horace Gregory's face harden as the man spotted him and he reined to a halt.

"I can't believe what I've been hearing, Fargo," Gregory snapped.

"What's that?" Fargo asked blandly.

"You hiring out to those damn fool Keegans. I'm really surprised."

"I am, too, in a way." Fargo smiled pleasantly. "But they made me a good offer."

Horace Gregory's gravelly voice stayed hard. "You've made a mistake, throwing in with those two crazy females," he said.

"They hired me. That's not throwing in with them," Fargo said.

"It comes out the same to most people," the man said.

"Can't see why," Fargo said.

"You're giving their wild ideas support by hiring out to them," Gregory said.

"Why does it bother you so? You've got your mail route. I thought that's what interested you," Fargo said.

"Their damn fool talk interests me. I want them shut up and away from here, as do most folks. You're not helping that by hiring out to them," the man said. "Working for them only makes you a part of their lies."

"Only if you see it that way," Fargo said calmly.

"That's the way a lot of people see it," Gregory almost shouted.

"Too bad." Fargo shrugged. The man's lips bit down on each other as he spun, strode to his horse and rode away, almost in a gallop. His men followed.

Fargo moved the pinto down the street and rode from the other end of town. He circled, climbed a steep hillside that let him look down on the lush thickness of the greenery of the hills and valleys. A glance at the sun told him it would be dark before he could bring Will Stedman back for a look at the horses in Gregory's corral and he made a note to do it first thing in the morning. He brought his gaze back to the terrain below. Profuse as it was, it couldn't hide a band of men on horseback. But it could hide a man on foot, he mused, letting his thoughts form of themselves. Or even two, especially in the dark of night.

He pondered the thought for a moment and made a face. Two men on foot might start the horses off, but they'd never be able to keep up with them. The herd would dissipate, run off in all directions after their first flight. To rustle a herd, you had to get them started and then drive them. He put aside the idea of men on foot. But not entirely. He realized he couldn't put anything aside entirely.

He turned the Ovaro downhill as the sun began to move behind the high hills. It was dark when he reached town.

He halted at the inn to freshen up in his room. The clerk stopped him as he entered. "One of the girls from the dance hall was here looking for you," the man said, adding a wink. "She said to meet her at the side door at nine o'clock."

"That'd be a half hour from now," Fargo said with a glance at the tall grandfather clock in the hall. He went to his room, used the washbasin to wash, and changed into a fresh shirt.

He reached the narrow alley at the side of the dance hall a few minutes before nine o'clock and the big Colt was in his hand. He had become unpopular to a lot of people, it seemed, and his antenna was raised. An alley ambush was an old ruse and he halted at the corner of the building opposite the dance hall. The alley was dark, but moonlight lent a pale glow to the street beyond the other end. Fargo dropped to one knee, scraped loudly with one boot as he held the Colt raised and ready to fire. But nothing moved at the other end of the alley. No gunslingers darted from around the corner to blast bullets up the narrow space.

Fargo scraped the heel of his boot along the ground again, but there was no response. He straightened up but kept the Colt in hand. He heard the side door to the dance hall open and he lifted the Colt instantly, but the figure that emerged had black-net stockings under a short skirt and almost black hair. Patty closed the door after her as she stepped toward him. "They're going to try to kill you," she whispered.

"Who?" he questioned.

"I don't know, but we were told to get you into bed in Room Three. That's in the rear on the ground floor," Patty said. "We were told to offer you a free ride, whoever you wanted."

"McAdoo's behind this."

"He told us what to do, but I think he was paid to do it," Patty said.

"Why do you think that?" Fargo asked.

"This isn't him. He's not smart enough to pull anything like this on his own. He wouldn't have the guts, either. But he'd horsewhip me if he knew I was here with you," Patty said.

"Why are you here?" Fargo queried.

"We all decided on it. The Keegan girls helped us. Now we've a chance to repay them," Patty said.

Fargo frowned into the night for a moment. "Is there another room next to number three?" he asked Patty and she nodded. "Make sure it's empty," he said and she nodded again. "Meanwhile, you play your part," he said and she slipped back through the doorway. He kept the gun in his hand as he stepped from the alley into the street, his eyes sweeping the buildings across from him, but there was only silence.

The Colt was back in its holster as he sauntered into the dance hall. McAdoo was at his usual spot at the corner of the bar and Fargo took a chair at a center table. He smiled inwardly. Perhaps McAdoo wasn't terribly smart or courageous, but he was canny. Fargo knew he'd have to play out his role, also, or the man would grow suspicious and perhaps alert the waiting killers. Patty came to the table and he ordered a beef sandwich, but no bourbon and sat back. She waited till he was finished and she cleared away the dishes. Then she returned, hands on her hips, and let her pelvis thrust forward provocatively. "I'm supposed to be offering you the free ride now," she said softly.

"Play it out," Fargo said and smiled, put his hand on her rear and felt its firmness. He nodded, exaggerating the movement so McAdoo couldn't miss it and he rose as Patty took him by the hand. "Go on. I'll be along in a minute," he told her and strolled to McAdoo with his eyes narrowed. "Why?" he slid at the man.

"Why what?" McAdoo answered.

"Why do I get a free ride?" Fargo asked and let suspicion cloud his face.

"Patty's got a real liking for you. It happens with the girls sometimes," McAdoo said.

"Where do you fit in?" Fargo questioned, still eyeing the man suspiciously.

"No place. Her ass, her decision. She wants to give it away, she has to make it double for me next time," the man said.

Fargo let his face soften and allowed a note of smug pride to come into his grin. "Guess some of us have it and some of us don't," and hurried to where Patty waited at a doorway that led to the rear of the dance hall.

"What was that all about?" she asked as she led him down a dim corridor.

"I had to seem a little suspicious. He'd expect that of me. He might've smelled a rat if I hadn't been," Fargo said. "But now he thinks everything's in order."

Patty halted before a doorway with the number three

painted on it and he followed her inside. A double bed took up half the room, one side against the wall with the room's lone window. A weathered old bureau rested against the left wall and a small lamp cast a dim glow. "Come on," he said, striding to the bed. "We've work to do."

"What if they come in on us?" the girl asked.

"They'll give us a little time, about fifteen minutes, I'd guess. They'll want us to be smack in the middle of enjoying ourselves," Fargo said as he lifted the bedspread and pushed the two pillows together end to end under it. He molded and fashioned the bedspread until it appeared as though two forms were underneath it. He and Patty looked at it as he stepped back.

"It looks right enough," she said, and he turned the lamp off.

"They won't be taking any long look," he said. "Now let's get into the next room." She led the way in to a room that was almost identical to the other one, and closed the door. A lamp burned dimly as she faced him.

"What now?"

"We wait," Fargo said. "When the shooting starts, you stay safe in here until it's over."

She smiled, an unexpected softness in it. "I'm sorry there isn't time," she said. "I'd like to give you that free ride, Fargo."

"Thanks for the thought. I'll take a rain check," he said as he put his ear to the door. He kept it there as he watched Patty lower herself to the edge of the bed. A frown crossed her brow. "What is it?" he asked.

"I just realized something," she said. "When they barge in to kill you, chances are they'll just blast away. That means they'd likely kill me or whatever girl you picked to go with."

"Chances are," he agreed.

"That bastard," she said through clenched teeth and he had no need to ask who she meant. "He had to know that."

"Naturally," Fargo said.

"Wait till I tell the other girls," Patty said. "Maybe it's time we did something about him."

"Such as?" Fargo asked.

"I don't know. But something. We'll be talking about it after this. You can be sure of that," she said.

Fargo smiled and kept his ear to the door. Not more than ten minutes had passed when he heard the footsteps outside— slow, cautious steps. More than one, but he couldn't tell how many. He drew the Colt as he closed his other hand around the knob of the door. Patty's eyes were on him, her body tense.

"Curtain going up," he said. The sharp sound of a door being smashed open came on the heels of his words. A volley of gunshots followed. At least three six-guns firing, he guessed. He yanked the door open, dropped to one knee as he spun into the hallway. The Colt was up and aimed as the two men came bolting from the room. "Drop the guns," he said, aware that it was most probably an empty offer. He was right. They whirled, starting to bring their guns up and he fired two shots with hardly a split second between them. Both men went into a quivering backward flip as they fell and Fargo's eyes were on the door as the third man came out partway and stared at his two companions for a second, surprise flooding his face.

He turned his glance, saw Fargo and threw himself back into the room. Fargo held his fire. He wanted the man alive and able to answer questions. He stayed low and darted into the room after the fleeing figure. He was in time to see the man throw himself through the window with a crash of glass.

"Damn," Fargo swore as he leaped onto the bed and ran to the window sill. The man was picking himself up from the ground and starting to run for three horses tethered a few yards away. Fargo vaulted through the window, hit the ground on both feet and fired again at the fleeing figure. He aimed the shot to slam into the ground at the man's feet.

But the man was too afraid to do anything but run. Fargo

holstered the Colt as he ran around the corner of the dance hall to where he'd left the Ovaro at the hitching post. He leaped into the saddle as he flipped the reins free and sent the horse into a gallop. He could hear the sound of the other horse racing through the night. The man cut through the center of town and raced up a steep hillside thick with red cedar. Fargo followed. He caught glimpses of his quarry as the man fled through the trees, but mostly he followed the sound of the horse crashing through brush. The powerful hindquarters of the Ovaro let him gain ground even uphill and when the slope flattened out, he heard the fleeing horse only a dozen yards ahead of him.

The sound changed direction. The man had veered to the right and Fargo swung the pinto after him. The brush grew higher, the tree cover heavier and he heard the horse ahead of him slowing. The drygulcher had made a mistake. Fargo smiled as he heard the horse only a few yards ahead of him now. Fargo peered through the blackness of the forest and caught a glimpse of the moving, dark bulk of the horse. He had pressed on another few feet when the shots rang out from the brush.

"Shit," he swore as he flung himself sideways from the saddle and felt one of the shots crease the collar of his shirt. He hit the ground hard and felt the breath go out of him. He'd been reckless, followed too eagerly and let himself be caught in a trap he'd used often enough himself. The man had jumped from the saddle as the horse kept going, hit the brush and lay in wait. Fargo swore at himself again and started to push up on his elbows as his breath returned only to see the figure rushing out of the brush at him, six-gun in hand. The man charged, plainly anxious to get as close to his target as he could. He fired off a shot that his haste sent slamming into the ground.

Fargo twisted the upper part of his torso and the next shot just missed his head. But the man was still coming forward, now carried by his own momentum. He tried to slow, but

Fargo's boot crashed into his ankle, the blow hard enough to make him stumble and another shot went wild. Fargo flung the lower part of his body sideways, sending his legs crashing into the man's ankles. The man went down, half falling and half stumbling. But Fargo had found the precious split seconds he needed, and he spun again as he yanked the Colt from its holster. He saw the man come up on one knee and raise his six-gun to fire. Fargo's fingers tightened on the trigger of his Colt. The gun barked and the man's body went backward, arching upward almost as though he were doing a back bend as the heavy bullet tore through his breast bone.

He dropped flat onto the ground with a dull thud and Fargo was instantly at his side. He was still alive. Fargo yanked him partway up by his bloodied shirtfront. "Who, damn you? Who sent you?" he shouted. He waited, watching the man's mouth fall open and his lips try to form words. But his last breath rushed from him in a gasped hiss and his jaw fell slack. "Damn," Fargo swore and let the lifeless form fall back onto the ground.

He stood up, whistled and the Ovaro came through the trees toward him. He swung onto the horse and a grimness rode with him back to town. The attempt on his life had failed, but the answer he'd wanted had eluded him.

Whoever tried to have him gunned down would know the attempt had failed when his gunslingers didn't report back. Or maybe he'd know firsthand, Fargo mused, thinking of Abe McAdoo. Of course, there'd been others in the dance hall who may have waited to see for themselves. He decided to stop by the dance hall just to see McAdoo's reaction for himself. And to let Patty know he was in one piece.

He drew up in front of the building, the murmur of voices from inside still strong. The two ambushers had been carted away by now, he knew. He pushed the doors to the dance hall open and paused for a moment to let his eyes sweep the room. A number of the men at the bar stared at him, most with respect and he saw Patty's eyes light up with relief. Abe

McAdoo stayed at his place at the end of the bar, his face expressionless as Fargo walked over to him.

"You always let your customers get dry-gulched?" Fargo asked.

"Wasn't my fault," the man protested.

"You had to see them come in," Fargo said.

"They said they were friends of yours, said they had to see you. I told them where you were," McAdoo said.

Fargo half-shrugged and seemed to accept the explanation as he turned away. The man was a smooth liar, Fargo muttered inwardly and he was at the door when Patty came up to him. "Thank God you're all right. I was afraid," she said, her voice low.

"Thanks," Fargo said.

"McAdoo asked me what happened. I told him you had real good ears and heard them at the door and you were ready when they came in," the girl said. "He bought it."

"Good going," Fargo said. "I'll stop by. Meanwhile, be careful."

"I will. We all will. The other girls know now how low he was willing to go. They all knew he was no good, but nobody thought he was that rotten," Patty said and Fargo saw the cold fury in her eyes.

Two of the other girls had come up and were listening and their eyes matched Patty's. Fargo walked from the room thinking that Abe McAdoo was a man in more trouble than he realized. But he was convinced that Patty's evaluation of him had been pretty much on target. McAdoo was a weasel of self-serving unscrupulousness, a man small in mind and spirit. He was a player, not a planner. Somebody else had done the planning and assigned him his role—somebody with more scope and evil imagination. Horace Gregory came to mind at once as Fargo swung onto the pinto and rode to the stable. Gregory was capable of planning. But had he been behind what had almost happened? Either he was maligned, a victim of Mary and Bonnie's unsupported conclusions, or he was everything they said and more—ruthless, clever and dangerous. Gregory was one that bore more watching. Fargo reminded himself to fetch Will Stedman come morning. He saw to the horse and returned to the inn, glad to welcome sleep.

He was in the saddle at sunrise and surprised Will Stedman when he arrived at the man's spread. "Get a mount. I want you to check on some horses with me," Fargo said. He explained more as he rode from the ranch with Stedman. "Think you could recognize the horses as yours?" he asked.

"I think so. They wouldn't be like horses I've had for years. The mounts we round up and saddle-break we ship on as soon as we can. But I think I'd know," the man answered with honesty. "I heard you were in a shootout in town last night," he slid at Fargo.

"News sure travels fast around here." Fargo smiled.

"It just happened that two of my boys were in town last night and told me about it this morning." Stedman laughed. "They didn't know any details, just that there was a shoot-out."

"Somebody tried to get rid of me," Fargo said and told him what had happened.

"Somebody's getting nervous," Stedman commented.

"Looks that way," Fargo agreed as he led the way up a slope onto a high path in a stand of red cedar. He rode the ridged forest land until they neared Gregory's place and then moved downward. But he kept inside the tree cover and reached a spot tha let them look down over Gregory's spread. Fargo felt the oath rise up in his throat as he stared down at the corrals. They were empty except for a few mustangs in one of the back corrals. He spied Horace Gregory near the compound with the dogs. "Damn, he's cleared them all out," Fargo muttered. "Sent them on their way."

"He has that," Stedman grunted.

"Damn, I'm sorry for the wild goose chase," Fargo apologized.

"Not your fault," Stedman said. "You just keep trying. Come visit anytime you feel it's in order."

Fargo nodded with grim appreciation and stayed as Will Stedman turned his horse and started back through the trees. Fargo stared at the ranch below for a few moments longer. Gregory could have moved the horses yesterday. There was enough light left for a few hours riding after Fargo had seen the herd in the corrals. Or he could've started them out at sunrise. Either way, no horses, no answers. Fargo's eyes scanned the scene below and saw a half-dozen hands in view. It was plain that Gregory didn't bother to drive his horses himself. He let half his crew take them while he stayed back with the other half.

Perhaps to round up fresh stock. Round up or rustle? The question poked itself at Fargo again and another thought crowded on its heels. A man driving a herd to market normally went along to argue for the best price. Certainly if there was a horse auction involved. Bonnie's words rose up inside him. Horace Gregory's horses never showed up at the horse sales. The thought stayed as he watched Gregory go into the compound. But another thought speared at him. Horace Gregory was too big to be a phantom. The same went for his hands. Yet horses weren't rustled by themselves. There had to be riders, even if they were ghost riders.

He turned the Ovaro around and rode slowly back through the cedars and turned toward Mary and Bonnie's place. Somebody had tried to kill him last night. He'd warn them to be extra alert.

7

The sun had passed the noon sky when he reached the sturdy frame-house in the hollow. He saw the door hanging open as he approached, and kept the pinto at a walk as he watched for one of the young women to appear. But neither had come to the doorway as he reined to a halt in front of the house and he felt a furrow touch his brow. "Anybody home?" he called out and received only silence. The furrow became a frown. They weren't the kind to go away and leave their door open.

He dismounted with a stab of uneasiness and as he stepped toward the doorway his hand rested on the butt of the big Colt. "Mary? Bonnie?" he called as he stepped through the doorway and into the house. This time he heard a sound, from one of the back rooms, a thumping noise. He moved forward, the Colt in his hand now, followed the sound and stepped into the bedroom and halted to stare at Bonnie. Bound onto a straight-backed chair, arms tied to the back, her eyes were wide with relief as they peered at him over the top of a wide cloth gag around her mouth. She was still rocking the chair from side to side to make the thumping sound and stopped when he entered.

"Christ," he muttered and he was at her side in three long strides. He took the gag from her mouth.

Words tumbled from her in a rush of breath. "Oh, God. Oh, dear God," she breathed.

"Who?" he asked as he began to untie the ropes that bound her arms behind the chair.

"Six men," she said. "One came to the door asking directions. We stepped outside to help him and the other five came out of the brush with their rifles at us."

"Where's Mary?" he asked as her arms came loose and he started to untie her ankles.

"They took her," Bonnie said. "Goddamn them, they took her."

"Why?" he asked as the last of the ropes came loose and Bonnie stood up. She swayed for a moment and he caught her.

"To make us stop. So we'd fire you," she said. "They said if I sent you on your way they'd return Mary alive. If I didn't, they'd kill her."

"How would they know?"

"They said they'd send somebody to find out in a few days," Bonnie told him as she rubbed circulation back into her wrists.

"That's all a crock of shit," Fargo said grimly. "Mary will be dead by then. And once they're sure you sent me on my way, they'll kill you."

Bonnie stared back. "You can't be sure of that."

"You think they could afford to leave either of you alive after this? They tried to kill me and didn't. This is another way to get rid of me and then both of you," he said and she uttered a groan of despair. "I'll try to pick up their trail. Six of them, you said?" Fargo asked.

"No, you can't!" Bonnie exploded. "They said if you followed them they'd kill Mary right away. If they see you, she's dead."

Fargo took Bonnie by the shoulders, his words harsh but his voice gentle. "If I don't get to her in time, she's dead. It's the only chance. They're just making threats to get you to do what they want—keep me off their tail and get rid of me," he told her.

"Then I go with you," Bonnie said. "You can't stop me from doing that."

He thought for a moment and shrugged. It was her right. But he had to make sure she understood. "I can't look out for you and try to save Mary," he said.

"I know," she said. "Thanks for being honest."

"When did they take her?" Fargo asked.

"Last night," Bonnie said.

He turned and she followed him outside to where he searched the ground at the perimeter of the hollow, his practiced gaze scanning every inch of the ground. He picked up the tracks at the south side of the hollow, knelt down and counted the hoofprints, seven horses in all. He rose, nodded to Bonnie and she hurried off to return on the Appaloosa, a rifle in a saddle holster and a five-shot, single-action Joslyn Army revolver stuck in the waistband of her riding skirt.

He climbed onto the Ovaro and she fell in behind him as he followed the line of hoofprints. The men had gone into single file almost at once, threading their way through the heavy foliage, probably with Mary in the center of the line. They had moved southward and stayed in the hill country until the land folded itself downward to become gently rolling plateaus heavy with bur oak, hackberry and box elder. The day was beginning to come to a close when he dismounted and ran his fingers over the tracks in the ground. "They're fresher. They didn't hurry and we've made good time," he said.

"Think we can catch up to them tomorrow?" Bonnie asked.

"If it goes as well as it did so far," he said. "They're keeping on a track, heading someplace. And they don't figure they're being followed." He swung back onto the pinto and as the night fell, found a half-circle of oak where the branches were low. He made a small fire to take the chill from the night and brought out the beef jerky he had in his saddle-bag. When they finished eating, Bonnie stepped behind the

Appaloosa and changed into a cotton nightdress with a scoop neck that let the edge of her high, round breasts show. He had undressed to underdrawers and lay on his bedroll when she settled down beside him, her eyes taking in his muscled beauty.

"It has to be Gregory," she murmured. "I know it."

"There's no proof, not yet," he said.

"The hell with proof. I know it," Bonnie said and he didn't answer. The coincidences were growing stronger as they circled in his mind. Gregory had moved the horses at the same time Mary was taken, two moves that really resulted in one thing: his not being able to pursue either trail. Clearly, that was the objective somebody wanted and that somebody was getting to look more and more like Horace Gregory. It was still not proof. There were still too many other strange, unexplained elements. But maybe Bonnie was right, Fargo grunted. The hell with proof. Knowing was what counted.

He glanced at her. She was sitting, her eyes still taking in his muscled symmetry. "Go to sleep. I want to be riding come sunrise," he said. She lay down, turned her back to him and he heard the soft, even breathing of sleep in moments.

He closed his eyes, also, and slept soundly until the first gray dawn light woke him. A small stream let him wash up and he waited while Bonnie took her things to the water. When she returned, she wore a fresh, light-yellow shirt. She could look more than ordinarily attractive, he decided. She rode beside him as he set out following the hoofprints again. The six horsemen with Mary had taken an almost straight trail southward, but their prints told him they had increased their pace—hoofmarks bit deeper into the ground.

Their quickened pace had lengthened their lead. The day was beginning to slide to an end when he slowed where a low hill of heavy cottonwoods rose. A glance at the ground showed him prints with the edges still moist and the trail led up the hill through the trees. Fargo reined to a halt. "They could be just over the other side of that hill," he said. "You stay here under this cedar while I have a look."

She nodded and climbed from the Appaloosa as he put the pinto into a trot up the hillside. He was into heavy tree cover at once and slowed, letting the horse pick its way through the trees and the tall brush. The right side of the hill curved upwards steeply and he glimpsed a half-dozen cave openings as he rode, most almost covered by tall brush and trees.

He kept to the center of the hillside and finally reached the top to see a wide plain stretch out where the tree line ended. A dozen or so clusters of hackberry dotted the plain and he saw the small knot of figures beside one of the near clusters. They were all dismounted. He saw Mary with her hands tied behind her back. He strained his eyes at her. She seemed all right, no pain or bruises on her face and he let his eyes move over the six men. Ordinary hands, he decided and as he watched, he saw three more horsemen approaching from the plain. Fargo edged the Ovaro closer to the end of the cottonwoods and watched the three riders halt and dismount. One man stepped forward and took a moment to look at Mary. The others stepped back respectfully. He was obviously the boss. He was a tall and lean figure, with a face that had a wolflike sharpness to it with a long nose, tight skin and black hair slicked straight back.

Too far away to hear, Fargo watched as the man spoke to Mary and then, with unexpected fury, slapped her across the face. Mary's reaction was a kick that landed on his knee and he dropped to the ground in pain. Fargo faintly heard his shouts and two of the others punched Mary in the stomach and threw her to the ground. The man with the wolflike face rose to his feet, flexed his knee and glimaced in pain. Mary stayed on the ground, though Fargo saw her raise her head. It was only then that he realized he had the Colt in his hand. He'd drawn it by reflex as they had started to punch Mary, ready to pour bullets into them if he had to. He dropped the gun back into its holster. They weren't ready to do more to Mary for now. He watched her push up to a sitting position.

Fargo had brought his gaze back to the wolflike man when he saw the sudden movement in the distance. His gaze stayed on it, saw it take shape and form and become a herd of horses moving toward him. He was frowning as the herd drew closer, and he made out six riders keeping some twenty horses together. Were these the horses from Gregory's corral, he wondered. He couldn't be sure, but it was plain that the riders and the ones who'd taken Mary had come to meet at the spot. The dusk began to drift down as the riders moved the herd to where a line of cedars bordered the trees from where he watched. They strung a loose rope corral that kept the horses more or less together. Fargo saw the others lift Mary to her feet and move to where the riders had begun to settle down. They were going to spend the night, Fargo realized as he watched the men unsaddle their horses. Mary, hands still behind her back, was tied to a thin sapling. He marked the spot in his mind, a dozen or so yards from the horses.

Dusk was fast turning into dark as Fargo backed the Ovaro from the edge of the trees. He kept the horse at a walk and went into a trot only when he started down the side of the hill. Bonnie was pacing back and forth when he reached her.

"They're camped on the other side of the hill," he said. "Mary's with them. So is a herd of horses. They obviously planned to meet there."

"Then we can go get her," Bonnie said.

"Whoa, not so fast. There are a dozen or so men there," Fargo said. "You ever see this man Rossand?"

"Once."

"Long nose, tight skin, sharp-faced with hair slicked back straight?" Fargo asked.

"That's him," Bonnie said.

"The horses have to be from Gregory's," Fargo thought

aloud, remembering how Will Stedman had confirmed that Gregory dealt with Rossand. "But that still doesn't prove he rustled them."

"I know, a man's got a right to round up wild horses," Bonnie snapped. "When do we go after Mary?"

"Just before dawn, when they'll all be sound asleep. They might post a sentry, but I don't think so. They're sure they won't be followed. We won't be taking any chances, though," he said and took his bedroll from the Ovaro. He stretched it on the ground and settled down on it. "We'll have most of the night to wait. Might as well rest some," he said and Bonnie lowered herself beside him to sit cross-legged. An almost full moon rose to bathe the ground in its silvery softness and he saw Bonnie studying him.

"It could go wrong, couldn't it?" she said matter-of-factly.

"There's always a chance of that," he agreed. She nodded gravely and he watched her turn to look out at the moonlit night. A warm wind blew fitfully and the night was quiet, the trees at their back a soft, dark wall and the flicker of fireflies gave a mischievous sparkle to the darkness. "What are you thinking?" he asked Bonnie.

"How pretty it is here," she said.

"Under other circumstances it'd be right romantic," he said.

She turned to him, uncrossed her legs and leaned down beside him. "What's wrong with these circumstances?" she murmured and suddenly her lips were against his, very soft and pliant. Her kiss lingered and then she drew back.

"In case something goes wrong?" he asked. "A last moment of pleasure?"

"No," she said. "Something I've been wanting to do."

He shrugged. He'd go with either reason and his arms came up around her and pulled her face down to his again. This time Bonnie's kiss was both soft and demanding, lips opening, enveloping, her tongue darting out, circling. He felt her hands pulling buttons open. He helped her and then yanked off his gunbelt and Levis and in moments he was naked beside her. The moonlight bathed her in its soft silvery glow, her breasts were indeed very round and very full. Not large, but deliciously shaped and a good spread of rib below them gave her a slightly barrel-chested torso. A little rounded belly, only slightly convex, added to the vibrant sensuality of her body and a small but very thick little triangle narrowed to where it met strong, firmly fleshed legs. He brought his mouth down to a pink nipple centered on a very large pink aureola and Bonnie's hands instantly dug into his back. "Ah, Jeez . . . ah, ah, good," she gasped out as his tongue caressed the pink tip, pulling the very round mound deeper into his mouth.

"Yes, oh, Jeez, yes," she moaned and he felt her arms tighten around his neck. He let his hand travel slowly down the round chest, caress the convex little belly and push through the very thick triangle. His fingers halted in the fibrous softness, explored, and felt the swell of her pubic mound, very rounded and full. Anatomical echoes, he found himself thinking—breasts and pubic mounds, fullness, roundness, softness. His lips stayed on her breast and his hand slipped down farther and touched her thighs still held together. "Oh, ooooh," Bonnie moaned and her thighs fell open and he felt her pubic mound push upwards, torso rising in invitation.

His hand came around the moist opening and felt the wetness of her and Bonnie cried out again. Her cry became a low, long moaning sound as he explored, touched, caressed dark and wet walls and he felt his own excitement at the touch of her. Her vibrant body quivered with tiny spasms as he touched deeper and little half-screams interrupted the low moans. "There, there, oh, God, there," Bonnie cried out and he obeyed, caressing the very tip of the malleable lips. Her fingers dug into his back and her firm-fleshed thighs fell open, closed, fell open again. "Jeez, oh, God, I'll come,

I'll come," she screamed and her hands pulled at his hips. He brought his throbbing member over her, moving quickly to her fervid wanting, waiting croft, the shelter of shelters, home of homes.

Her legs tightened against him, firm thighs strong, and her body quaked and quivered, pulsed and pumped as he thrust deeply, stayed with her and she was screaming sounds of ecstasy. There was no soft subtlety with her, only an encompassing wildness. When he felt Bonnie's torso lift high and heard her screams begin to spiral, he was at his own very edge of delirious pleasure and he exploded with her, felt her tightening around him, her arms pulling his mouth to one round, full breast. "Aiiiiieeeeee . . . oh, oh, Jeeeeez . . . oh, yes, yes, damn, damn, damn," Bonnie screamed and quivered against him, her convex little belly thrust hard against his groin. Finally, her screams trailing away, he heard her shuddered sob that was still made of ecstasy. She pulled him hard against her as she fell back on the bedroll. Her breath came in little gasped sounds now and the round, full breasts moved up and down under his lips.

He stayed with her until finally she let him draw away and he rested on one elbow beside her. It had been a kind of echo, also, the senses echoing the flesh, this time, all of it as vibrant and sensual as her body beside him. She folded herself against him and he slept with her in the soft silence of the night. The moon had crossed to the far end of the sky when he felt her stir beside him and he woke to see her leaning over him. Her lips brushed his cheek. "Be right back. Nature calls," she murmured and he watched her round, firm little rear disappear into the trees.

He lay back a moment more to gather his thoughts. There was a little more than an hour of darkness left, he estimated, more than enough time to get Mary. With caution and luck, he reminded himself. He turned his head to see Bonnie hurrying back, the last of the moonlight giving her a ghostly loveliness, her high, round breasts bouncing ever so slightly.

She dropped to her knees beside him, her arm coming around and he felt the curse form in his throat. He saw the heavy rock in her hand and tried to twist away, but she was too quick. It came down on his head, just back of his temple and the world spun for an instant, faded into grayness and then there was nothing.

He lay still on the bedroll, oblivious to Bonnie pulling on clothes and hurrying to the Appaloosa. She left a few moments later and he knew nothing until the first stirrings. Faint feelings. Sensation returning. Throbbing over his temple, then grayness replacing the void and he pulled eyes open, blinked and his last moment of awareness swept through him. He pushed up on both elbows and saw the piece of paper beside him on the bedroll. He picked it up and turned it so the moonlight fell on the words pencilled on it.

"I'm sorry. If they see you they'll kill Mary. I can't take that chance. I've got to save her myself. At least they won't kill her if they should see me. Thanks for bringing me this far. Bonnie."

"Damn fool girl," Fargo swore as he leaped to his feet and pulled on his clothes. In minutes he was on the pinto and climbing the hill, moving slowly through the blackness of the thick foliage. He veered the horse to his right when he was a little more than halfway up the hillside, his thoughts rushing ahead, anticipating the worst and unhappily aware he was not being pessimistic. He found one of the caves, its pitch-black mouth almost impossible to see. He dismounted, led the horse inside and paused for a moment to listen. But he heard no sounds. The cave was empty and he dropped the reins onto the ground some six feet inside the inky blackness.

The Ovaro would stay, he knew, unless he was called out or cornered by wolves or a bear. Fargo left the cave in a loping run, his body crouched over as he made his way up the rest of the hill.

When he reached the top, he saw the glow of flames. The men had a campfire going. He edged his way to the end of the tree line. The fire had been fed by two fresh logs, he noted, most of the men standing in a half-circle around it. He also saw something else: Bonnie was held by two men as Rossand stood in front of her. Fargo's eyes went to the sapling and saw Mary still tied to it. He moved along the edge of the trees, circled to the side of the campsite where the cedars extended almost to the rope corral that had been drawn around the horses.

He crept closer, to the very edge of the last two cedars. He could see and hear plainly now and winced at the open-handed blow Rossand smashed against Bonnie's face. "You're lying, bitch," the man snarled, his voice reedy and high in pitch.

"No, I came alone," Bonnie said and Fargo saw the hate in her eyes that gave her the strength of defiance.

"Bullshit. You couldn't have tracked us this far. You had that goddamn Trailsman with you," Rossand said and hit her again.

"No," Bonnie shouted back.

He hit her again. "Where is he? Where'd you leave him?" Rossand demanded.

"In Hillsdale," Bonnie said. "Bastard," she added.

Rossand spun to the men standing by. "We're wasting time. He's got to be near, probably in the trees watching us or hiding on the hill. Three of you stay here with me. The rest of you go find the bastard."

The men hurried to their horses and Fargo watched them ride away. They'd make a sweep up and across the hillside and then down through the trees that led to the camp. He was glad he'd hidden the Ovaro in the cave. The two men holding Bonnie threw her on the ground alongside Mary and bound her wrists with a length of lariat. Fargo's eyes moved across the campsite and spied Bonnie's Appaloosa near the other horses inside the ropes. His eyes returned to Rossand as the man stared at Bonnie and Mary. There were only three men besides Rossand. It seemed the best time to go after the girls. He could probably bring down Rossand and the other three with one fast volley of shots.

But the others would certainly hear it. They'd come charging back just as he was untying the girls. And if he could somehow distract Rossand and the three others long enough to free Mary and Bonnie, he'd still run head-on into the searchers as they swept through the trees. No, ridiculous as it seemed, his only chance was to wait for everyone to return. For Rossand, there was only one thing of real importance: the horses. Fargo felt certain everything else was secondary. He counted on that. Freeing Mary and Bonnie depended on his being right. He settled down to wait after a quick glance at the sky. The moon was vanishing over the distant hills. He had another half hour of darkness left at best, and he swore softly as he waited.

Not more than another ten minutes had passed when the searchers rode out of the trees and dismounted near the fire. One man stepped forward to Rossand. "Nothin'," he said. "We made a good sweep from the bottom of the hill. We'd have spotted him or his horse for sure. I think she was tellin' the truth. She managed to trail us."

Rossand's face showed displeasure, but he shrugged. "We'll be moving on in an hour," he said and turned away to settle himself down near the fire. Fargo watched the others lower themselves to the ground to catch another hour of sleep.

He rose to a crouch, moved to his right through the trees and then stepped from the tree cover when he was on the other side of the herd of horses. He drew closer to the herd and pulled the Colt from its holster. He halted at the back of the herd. Some of the horses already sensed his presence and moved restlessly. He pointed the barrel of the gun into the air and shattered the night with six shots, fired in clusters of two.

The herd bolted in panic, sweeping aside the thin ropes with their charging bodies and pounding hooves. Fargo dropped to one knee and reloaded as he heard the shouts of surprise and alarm.

Rossand's voice rose above the others. "Myers, stay here with the two bitches. Everybody else after the goddamn horses," the man shouted.

Fargo dropped flat on his stomach as he saw Rossand spin and peer into the darkness trying to pick out a fleeing figure where the herd had been. The man spun again, ran to his horse and raced after the others. Fargo saw the guard left behind move closer to Mary and Bonnie. But Fargo found a grim smile. He had guessed right. The horses were the all-important thing to Rossand, much more so than two females who could be dealt with at another time if need be. Fargo brought his gaze back to the guard. The man had his revolver in hand as he peered nervously into what remained of the night.

Fargo remained flattened on the ground as the man slowly turned, his eyes moving in a circle, his arm half-raised to fire. As the man turned to peer across the other side of the plateau, Fargo's hand whipped down to the leather sheath around his calf and he drew the thin, double-edged throwing knife often called an Arkansas toothpick. He waited a moment more, let the man turn away from him. Then he rose, took a second to aim and sent the thin, shaft hurtling through the night. He heard the man's gagging sound as the knife slammed into the base of his neck, almost between his shoulder blades. The man took three staggering steps forward, but Fargo was already up and racing across the ground.

He reached Mary and Bonnie just as the man pitched forward onto his face. Fargo yanked the knife from the twitching figure, wiped it across the back of the man's shirt and turned to Bonnie and Mary. They stared at him with relief in their round eyes. He cut Mary's ropes and pulled her to her feet and spotted her horse tethered to a tree a dozen yards away. "Get your mount. It won't take them long to catch the herd and come back," he said and turned away.

"Fargo!" The cry came from Bonnie and he paused to look back at her. "Dammit, untie me," she said.

"I'm still thinking about it," he said and she blinked back. "I ought to fan your little ass," he growled. "There's no time. That's the only thing that's stopping me."

"I'm sorry," she murmured.

He bent over and cut her bonds and she leaped to her feet and ran to the Appaloosa near where Mary had climbed onto the bay. The two young women followed him as he went into his long, low loping run and led the way into the trees. He made better time on foot through the thick tree cover than they did. The first faint light of dawn was beginning to filter through the top branches when he turned and ran to the caves at the side of the slope. He halted, whistled and the Ovaro trotted out of the nearest cave. Fargo swung onto the horse and rode down the remainder of the hillside as the morning sun peeked over the distant hills. When they reached the flat land, he let the horses drink at a small pond.

"We going to circle around and follow them?" Mary asked as she dismounted to walk to where he waited beside the pinto.

"No," Fargo said.

"Rossand's place is less than a day's ride south. I heard one of the men say so. We'll be able to see his operation," Mary said.

"That won't help us, not by itself," Fargo said and they both frowned back. "We still need proof that Gregory's supplying him with rustled horses. Gregory or somebody. We don't even know how that's done with these phantom rustlers. Seeing Rossand's spread won't do that for us.

Finding out who's rustling the horses and how, is still the first step. We can't stop Rossand without that, and we can't nail Gregory for his part in it until we know what it is."

"What are you going to do now?" Mary asked.

"First, take you back to your place," Fargo said. She put her arms around him, resting her head against his chest.

"Thanks for coming after me," she said. "I can't ever really thank you for that."

"Maybe you did it already," he said into her ear and saw her little smile. "Let's get back," he said and swung into the saddle.

Bonnie came over from where she'd been a half-dozen feet away. "What are you going to do after we're back at our place?" she questioned.

"I'm going to see about phantom rustlers," he said.

"Will Stedman's sentries didn't see them. How do you expect to?" she asked.

"Stedman's men were positioned to look for rustlers," Fargo said.

"What are you going to be looking for?" Bonnie frowned.

"Ghosts," he said and laughed at their stares as he rode on.

8

The night was dark and still in the ravine only a mile or so from Will Stedman's ranch. Fargo's glance traveled up the sides of the ravine, thick with wiry brush and hackberry. He had picked out a tree, a wide-trunked old-timer with low branches he could reach in one leap and now he relaxed on a patch of soft apple moss. The night before had been fruitless but an inner sense told him this night would be different. Rossand had taken a herd of horses to his place. He'd be needing more soon enough. It was time for his supplier to go into action. It was time for the phantom rustlers to strike again.

He thought back for a moment to Mary and Bonnie when he'd deposited them back at their place. They had been as belligerent as ever despite their brush with death. Perhaps more so, with new angers to feed their convictions. "You satisfied now that the mail route you blazed was only so he could spot herds?" Mary had pushed at him.

"No," he had said and they stared at him. "That's not enough reason by itself," he added and their faced softened. "It's being used for something else, but I'm damned if I know what."

"A fast trail for his rustlers," Bonnie said.

"A band of riders having to travel single file? No, that wouldn't be fast," Fargo said. "Besides, nobody's seen any rustlers, remember?"

"What then?" Mary queried.

"I don't know," he'd answered. "But I'm not eliminating anything."

"Such as?" Bonnie pressed.

"You two can't see anybody but Horace Gregory. Maybe you're right. He had me mark that route for him. A lot points to him, but you ever think that maybe he's not alone?" Fargo said to them. "Maybe Will Stedman's been driving his own horses. Maybe that's why his men haven't seen any rustlers. Maybe they've said what they were ordered to say."

Fargo smiled as he remembered the astonishment in both their faces. It was plainly something they had never considered. "Stedman supplying Rossand, too," Mary had finally breathed. He had nodded agreement at the possibility.

"No, I don't believe that," Bonnie had cut in sharply. "Not Will Stedman. I can't believe that at all."

"And I can't believe in phantom rustlers," Fargo said.

"You saw the mustangs in our valley race off, nobody chasing them," Bonnie reminded him.

"They could've been spooked on their own," Fargo had answered.

"So often? You admitted that wasn't likely," Bonnie had tossed back. "Truth is, Fargo, you've got nothing except phantom rustlers, believe in them or not."

Fargo snapped his thoughts off. He had left the women then, aware of words that were uncomfortably true. They certainly stayed with him as he stretched out in the ravine. He let himself catnap—periods in which he was never fully asleep—and the night wore on.

The moon had made its wandering way across the sky when he felt his body grow tense. The sound came through the ground before he actually heard it, a pounding vibration and then his ears picked it up as he pushed to his feet. It was hooves thudding into the ground. The sound grew louder, filling the ravine with a speed he hadn't expected and he started running as he saw the tremendous dark mass came into sight, moving toward him. He raced across the ground toward the side of the ravine and the dark mass took shape, became thundering, charging bodies and pounding hooves.

The trees at the side of the ravine suddenly seemed very far away as he dug heels into the soil. The charging herd was close enough for him to feel the heat of its breath as he reached the tree. He flung himself upward, caught the lowest branch and pulled his legs up, curling himself around the thick limb to see the herd roaring past. He peered down the ravine to the end of the herd, searching for riders chasing after the racing horses. But he saw no figures on horseback, no riders closely chasing the herd or hanging back. No one. Nobody, he repeated. Not one damn rider. His eyes went back to the herd charging past so close he could almost reach out and touch them.

It was then that he almost fell off the tree branch in astonishment. He knew he was staring open-mouthed as the last horse raced by, his eyes riveted on the furry forms that ran at the rear of the herd. He continued to stare, transfixed and counted a dozen: the German shepherds came first, the border collies along the sides and the larger Bernese mountain dogs spread out the rear. The shepherds bit and nipped at the legs of the horses as they ran, deftly avoiding flying hooves and biting quickly into a hock or even a flank. The border collies running alongside the herd kept the horses from spreading out, herding them together from both sides and the Bernese mountain dogs raced back and forth to bring up those that fell back or tried to stray. But most remarkable of all, the pack worked in absolute silence, with flashing fangs and quick, darting movements that drove the herd onward.

Gregory's dogs, Fargo bit out silently. The phantom rustlers. Working as a pack and individually, driving the herd with silent efficiency. All but hidden by the horses and the darkness. It was no wonder Stedman's sentries hadn't seen them. Nor had Fargo seen them as they drove the mustangs from the valley as he watched with Mary. So much was suddenly explained. Fargo grimaced as he dropped from the tree branch and ran to where he had hidden the Ovaro in a cluster of hackberry. The fleeing herd had already gone out of sight as Fargo leaped into the saddle and sent the pinto after them. But he followed by sound and took care to stay back.

The horses continued on through the ravine, were herded into a narrow gulley and then into an adjoining ravine. He could hear their progress and he quickened his own pace not to fall too far behind. He came in sight of the herd. Gregory's dogs were continuing to drive the horses with silent effectiveness. Horses instead of sheep or cows, Fargo grunted. Simple, yet not at all simple. Gregory had his talents, used for the wrong ends, but nonetheless there. Fargo suddenly pulled back on the reins. The herd was drawing closer to Horace Gregory's place and a band of horsemen appeared, moving down from the hills. Fargo drew to a halt and watched them take charge of running the horses with cracking whips and shouts and Fargo stayed where he was. He had seen all of it, now—the phantom, four-legged rustlers beginning the job and when they had the horses close enough to Gregory's place, his men took over to drive them into corrals.

Fargo turned the Ovaro around and climbed a hillside, rode deeper into the high land and found a spot to bed down under a cottonwood. The night still had a few hours left and he'd use them to sleep. Tomorrow would bring time to make plans and ride hard. He let the warm night wrap sleep around him and he woke only when the morning sun slid over the hills. He found a stream, washed and dressed and turned the pinto toward the hollow across the other side of the hills.

Mary and Bonnie were running from the house the moment they saw him ride up.

"Coffee?" Mary asked.

"Sounds great," he said and waited till he was at the kitchen table and had his first sips of the hot brew before he answered the questions that danced in their eyes. "No phantom rustlers," he said. "Just ones I've never seen before."

"Dammit, don't talk in riddles," Bonnie snapped and he laughed.

"Four-legged rustlers. Damn good ones, too," he said and quickly retold everything he had seen. Both stared at him with astonishment when he finished.

"My God, that explains everything," Mary said.

"The mail route, too," Fargo said. "I was right. It was a lot more than a way to spot herds. Bringing an entire pack of dogs through the hills would be real hard. Too many things to distract them, too many stray horses they might go after. He wanted to run them along a narrow trail that would keep them all together until he spotted the herd he wanted," Fargo explained.

"What now? We go get Gregory?" Bonnie asked.

"No. We've the proof we needed for him now. He can be picked up later. It's Rossand now. I know he's receiving stolen horses. When I find out what he's doing with them, maybe there'll be more to hang on him," Fargo said.

"We're going," Mary said. He started to protest but she cut him off. "This thing has been ours from the start. We're going to be in on the finish."

He met her firm gaze and turned a glance at Bonnie. "No more smartass moves," he rasped.

"Promise," she said.

"Get saddled." He nodded and had only minutes to wait before Bonnie returned on the Appaloosa and Mary on her bay. He set a fast pace out of the high hills and retraced the steps he'd taken when he'd followed Mary and her captors. When night fell he bedded down in a little arbor of box elder and Mary brought cold spiced chicken from her saddlebag.

"You owe us an apology, Fargo," she said as they ate. "We were right about Horace Gregory all along."

"Never said you weren't," he answered and drew cries of protest. "I said you'd no damn proof and you didn't, until I got it for you. So I wouldn't wait around for any apologizing."

They fell silent for the rest of the meal and he took down his bedroll and started to undress. They hurried to their saddlebags, went into the brush and returned in almost identical gray cotton nightgowns. Bonnie lay down on one side of him and Mary on the other. They fell asleep quickly, within minutes of each other and he embraced sleep also. He woke, hardly an hour later, to find Mary asleep against him on one side, Bonnie on the other. He returned to sleep with a smile.

When he woke in the morning he found Mary's arm around his chest and Bonnie's across his waist. They woke when he moved their arms, rose and found a stream. When everyone was in the saddle he set a hard pace with no time for conversation. By the time the day was at an end, they were in land that was relatively flat with wide strands of bur oak and cottonwoods. They had already passed the spot where he'd reached Mary and he found a place to stop for the night in a thicket of oak. When Mary and Bonnie appeared in their almost identical nightgowns he was resting on his bedroll and they came down beside him. "We ought to reach his place by noon," Fargo said. "According to what Mary heard."

"What happens when we get there?" Bonnie asked.

"We stay back, stay quiet and watch," Fargo said.

"Is that all?" Bonnie queried.

"There'll be a lot of them and three of us. That pretty much limits us to watching," Fargo said.

"I've limits on what I can watch," Bonnie said.

"Me, too," Mary said.

Fargo heard tiny alarm bells go off inside him. "Meaning exactly what?" he asked.

"I can't sit and watch him slaughter horses," Bonnie said. "I'll kill him."

"Me, too," Mary echoed.

Fargo felt more than uneasiness. He'd almost forgotten the tattered armor and dedicated banners. He'd almost forgotten how deep the roots of their causes were, deeper than anything so trivial as common sense. He suddenly realized he had to dampen down the short fuses burning inside the both of them. "You want to put a stop to Rossand and Gregory? You can't do it if you're dead. You've got to wait for the right time and do the right thing," he said.

"Such as?" they chorused.

"Go to the federal marshal at Stannardville with what you've found out. Let him take it from there," Fargo said.

"God knows how long that'd take," Bonnie snapped.

"It's the way to make it really stick," Fargo said.

"Rossand dead will make it stick," Bonnie said.

"Yes, but not us with him. I didn't come all this way to get myself killed because you two can't get a handle on your emotions," Fargo growled. "You hear me?"

"We hear you," they said as one and Fargo grunted, the answer far from satisfying. He lay back, closed his eyes and heard both girls stretch out, side by side this time. He slept, but far from well and they rode in silence with him as he set out in the morning. His quick glances saw the growing tightness in their faces. He suddenly realized the root of the tension inside them and decided to bring it into the open.

"You're afraid," he said and their eyes flashed to him. "You're afraid of what we'll find, what you'll have to see. You're afraid it'll hurt too damn much."

"Go to hell, Fargo," Mary muttered but the admission

was in her face. He glanced at Bonnie. She stared straight ahead and he smiled. He had hit home.

"You want to see but you don't want to see," he said. "Then stay back. I'll go and tell you what I found."

He watched Bonnie and Mary exchange glances. "No. We'll go along," Bonnie said, pride and determination overcoming the appeal of his suggestion. But he hadn't really expected differently and he put the Ovaro into a trot. They had gone perhaps another five miles when he slowed. A low incline with thick bur oak cut off their view, but not their sense of smell. The odor drifted to them on the heat of the afternoon sun, unmistakable, and slightly sickening—the heavy scent of meat being dried and meat turning bad, all mixed in with the odor of fresh blood and fresh kills.

His own jaw had grown tight as he nosed the horse up the incline and through the trees. The incline leveled off as the tree cover ended and a flat plateau stretched out in front of him. There were a half-dozen large buildings, barns and one house, plus four corrals. The first things Fargo saw were the racks of meat being dried in the sun, hanging from hooks attached to poles. Most of it was at least a week old, he guessed. But at the far side of one of the barns, he saw a horse on its side on the ground and four men starting to cut it apart with large saws. In the distance, beyond the last of the barns, he saw the skeletons and carcasses of three horses. He moved forward to the very edge of the trees and dismounted. Bonnie and Mary did the same.

Resting on one knee, the two young women beside him, he frowned as he watched the very busy operation. In one corral he saw a dozen cows and in another, over a dozen horses. But the busiest part of the operation was at the right side of a long roofed barn where men were carrying square slabs of dried meat from the building to six big Owensboro heavy drays with tall, chain-linked stake sides and extra diagonal braces on the rear axles—wagons meant for carrying heavy loads. Four of the wagons were already loaded with the big squares of dried meat and Fargo's gaze stayed on the wagon being loaded. He saw Rossand supervising the loading, his sharp, wolfish face carefully watching all that went on. The men had the wagon three-quarters loaded, in even layers of dried meat from the front to the rear when Rossand clapped his hands and pointed to the building adjoining the corral with the cows in it.

The men hurried to the building and soon emerged carrying more squares of dried meat which they placed on top of the meat already on the dray. They put on two layers which filled the wagon to the top and Fargo's eyes were narowed as he peered at the men lifting the last squares of meat onto the dray. "That's dried beef," he murmured. "They're putting two layers of beef on top of the horsemeat." His eyes were still narrowed as he watched the men start to load the sixth wagon with squares of meat from the other barn. "Back to the horsemeat," Fargo breathed. "They're filling the wagons with horsemeat and covering it with two layers of beef. Somebody's getting his ass cheated like crazy. Somebody's paying for beef and getting mostly horsemeat. On six wagons Rossand would be making thousands of extra profit. Beef's a hell of a lot more expensive than horsemeat."

He glanced at Bonnie and Mary. He knew they had heard him but they stared out at the scene in front of them, neither saying a word. Each had a tearstain, he saw. Fargo brought his eyes back to the spread. Rossand barked orders to his men as he continued to supervise the operation. It was plain they were going to move out with the six wagons as soon as the last one was loaded. Rossand was running an operation of grim and grisly efficiency. While he made a delivery with his big stake-sided drays, he had more sides of beef and horsemeat hung and drying, being prepared for when the wagons returned. Three men were sprinkling salt on already dried slabs of meat to further preserve it, Fargo saw. His eyes went to a sudden movement at the edge of the far corral. A man led a horse out of the enclosure and Fargo felt

Bonnie's arm move beside him. He glanced at her and saw the six-gun in her hand. She raised the gun to aim.

"No," he hissed and struck out to close his hand over hers before she could pull the trigger. But his hand hit against her and he heard the explosion of sound as the gun went off. "Goddammit, Bonnie," he swore.

"I wasn't going to shoot. I just wanted to get him in my sights," she said. He didn't know whether to believe her but he knew he could believe the explosion of activity at the ranch. Riders were already on horseback as Rossand, crouching by one of the drays, barked orders. Two bands of his men were racing toward the trees, one to come in from the right, the other from the left.

"Shit," Fargo spit out as he leaped onto the Ovaro and saw Bonnie starting to run to where the Appaloosa had backed off a few feet. Mary was on her feet, running to her horse when Fargo saw her stumble and go down.

"Dammit," he heard her curse as she pushed to her feet. But precious seconds had gone by and the riders were in the trees, coming at them from both sides. He saw the first of them as Mary pulled herself onto the bay and he whirled. The others were charging up from the other side. Fargo swore and pulled the Ovaro to a halt. Any wrong move would catch them in a cross fire.

The two bands of riders slowed as they came forward. "Throw your guns down," one of the men ordered. "Careful, now." Fargo dropped the Colt on the ground and saw Bonnie and Mary let their guns fall. "Let's go," the man said as one of the others dismounted to scoop up the guns. The riders surrounding them, they moved through the trees and into the open and Fargo saw Rossand standing, watching as his men brought their captives back.

Rossand turned a cold smile on Bonnie and Mary. "You two are like bad apples. You keep turning up," he said. His eyes went to the big man on the Ovaro. "Only now we have the famous Fargo with us," Rossand said, his voice heavy with disdain. "My lucky day." He motioned and Fargo dismounted, Mary and Bonnie following. Rossand stepped a pace closer, his tight-skinned face made of cruelty. "I'm sorry I haven't time to stay and enjoy killing all three of you, but I never let pleasure interfere with business. I have a schedule to meet. That means I must leave as soon as the last wagon is loaded." His eyes went to Fargo. "Too bad. I'd have enjoyed watching you carved up, a little at a time. I get very displeased with people who try to stop me from earning a living."

"Bastard," Bonnie hissed and Rossand turned to her.

"Enjoy these two," he said with a nod at the girls and a glance at the man alongside him. "I'm leaving five of you here as usual, Joey. And these two little ladies for you to enjoy. Pass them around as often and as long as you like. But I want them dead, along with Fargo, before I get back tomorrow night."

"Yes, sir, Mister Rossand," Joey said and Fargo saw the anticipation already forming in the man's face. Fargo swore silently as his mind raced to find some gleam of hope, some way out, but at the moment he didn't see any.

"Tie them up and put them in the barn, then finish your work before you start enjoying yourselves," Rossand said as he strode away. The sixth and last wagon was almost loaded, Fargo noted as he was led into the barn with Bonnie and Mary. The barn held more slabs of dried meat in the rear. As Joey stood by, six-gun in hand, two others took lengths of lariat to tie their prisoners. They took Fargo first, pulled his arms behind him and bound his wrists tightly. They turned to Bonnie and Mary and Mary held her wrists out.

"I've a sore shoulder. I don't want my arms pulled back," she said. The men looked at Joey and he nodded.

"Tie her hands in front," he conceded. When the men finished with Bonnie and Mary, they were pushed down to the floor against the side of the barn. Fargo was ordered to sit some six feet from them and his ankles were quickly bound. As he watched the men finish, his thoughts were on Mary. She no doubt did have a sore shoulder, probably from her last time as captive. She hadn't tried to be clever, but she had thrown him the ray of hope he'd been desperately trying to find. Joey stood in front of the men as they tied Mary's ankles. "Double tie her and double knot it," he ordered. That way it'll take her half the night to get loose and we'll be back long before that." He laughed and walked away when the men finished tying Bonnie. Fargo's eyes followed the men as they left and pulled the barn door almost closed.

But he could hear Rossand's voice as the man barked orders. He was ready to move. Fargo heard the horses being harnessed and soon after, the shouts of the team drivers and then the sound of wagon wheels turning, creaking with the weight of heavy loads. Rossand and his men were leaving—a driver and a helper with each wagon, he guessed. That made twelve right there and six left behind. That accounted pretty much for all of them, Fargo calculated. He turned his eyes to Bonnie and Mary and saw Bonnie watching him. "You hit my hand. I just wanted the feel of him in my sights. I wasn't going to shoot," she said defensively.

"How was I supposed to know that?" he snapped and her lips tightened. "You shouldn't have taken the gun out," he told her. That was truth, even if he had reacted too quickly.

"I wasn't going to shoot. You believe me?" she asked, her voice almost sulky.

"Doesn't matter. All that matters now is getting out of here," he said.

"There's no way," Marry muttered darkly.

"Yes, there is. I figure Joey and his friends will finish their chores, eat and maybe have a drink and then arrive to enjoy the rest of the night with you two. Then all day tomorrow," Fargo said.

"Dammit, we don't need it spelled out," Mary flared.

"That's to help keep your fingers from getting tired," Fargo said.

"What's that mean?" Bonnie frowned and he began to push his way across the floor to where they sat. He lifted his bound ankles and deposited them in Mary's lap.

"Use your fingers. Pull up my pants leg. Take the knife out of the calf holster," he said. She bent forward, using all ten of her fingers to lift his pants leg and he saw her eyes widen as she saw the double-edged throwing knife. She pulled it out and grasped in her fingers. He pulled his ankles out of her lap, swung himself around and pressed his bound wrists against her hands. "Start cutting," he said. "You'll only be able to make short cuts, but don't let that bother you."

He felt the ropes move ever so slightly as she began to cut with the edge of the blade.

"Little sawing motions," he said. "All you'll need is to get the top rope cut."

"Yes," she murmured and he heard her breathing hard as her head bent low against his back. He felt her sawing, her breath against him. "My fingers, they're going to fall off," she murmured. "I can't keep on."

"I figure you've another half hour," he said. "Then it won't be your fingers hurting."

"Shut up," she hissed savagely, but he felt the blade move back and forth again with renewed strength.

"Oh, God, oh, God," Mary gasped after another ten minutes. "My fingers are locked. They'll never open."

"They still holding the knife?" he asked and felt her nod. "Keep cutting," he said. "Dammit, keep cutting."

She was suddenly sobbing, soft sobs with soft curses mixed in. "Oh God, I hurt so. I can't go on, I can't," Mary gasped.

"Yes, you can, dammit. You're close. You have to be close," Fargo urged and heard her sobbing again but the blade continued to move.

"Come on, Mary, come on," he heard Bonnie whispering and his eyes went to the door. An hour had gone by, he guessed. They were on borrowed time and he felt the knife moving slowly, the small sawing motions coming to an end. Mary's sobs were a shuddered sound, nothing left inside them. She had done her best and he felt the blade brush his wrist as it fell.

"Damn," he swore, drawing his lips back as he gathered the strength of his powerful wrists and forearms. He pulled, feeling the veins in his neck stand out. Suddenly he felt something else, the rope shredding. He pulled again and it broke loose. He rubbed his wrists together and the rest of the rope loosened and he yanked his wrists free. He turned to look at Mary. She sat against the wall, holding her cramped fingers up, but her eyes were wide with hope. Fargo's attention turned back to the door as he heard the footsteps approaching. Fargo twisted his torso, his ankles still bound, found the blade on the floor and scooped it up. He slashed down with the edge, severing his ankle bonds with one stroke just as the barn door was pushed open.

"In here," Joey said as he entered. He froze for an instant when he saw the three figures huddled together. He snapped out of the moment and reached for his gun, but Fargo had used the precious second. Flinging the blade with a short underhand motion, he sent the knife whistling through the air in a straight, slightly upward path. It hurtled into the man's chest with full force, burying itself to the hilt. Joey, the gun in his hand, staggered backward on his heels. The gun dropped from his hand as he staggered out of the barn just as the four other men came up. They were staring at him as he fell onto his back. Then they saw the hilt of the knife blade protruding from his chest, almost as if it had suddenly sprouted there.

They stared for a moment and then turned away from Joey to race into the barn, drawing their guns as they did. But

Fargo was already running down the length of the big barn to the rear where the stacks of dried meat were piled in thick squares, with narrow passages between the stacks. He dropped low, saw the men start to spread out to search for him and he allowed a grim smile to touch his lips. Unarmed, the only chance he had was for them to stay separate. He crouched and his gaze swept the section of the barn where he'd paused. He uttered a silent cry of pleasure as he saw the pitchfork against the wall. He darted from behind one of the stacks of meat and seized hold of the tool. One of the searchers neared, moving cautiously through the passage to his left. Fargo cast a quick glance to his right and glimpsed two of the others moving along the other side of the barn. The pitchfork held in both hands, he crept forward, his eyes on the shadow of the man about to reach the end of the stack of meat. He took another step on the balls of his feet and was at the corner of the stack as the man rounded it.

Fargo plunged the pitchfork forward and saw all three of the prongs go into the man's belly. The man's mouth fell open as he gasped out a groaning cry and the gun fell from his hand, hit the ground and went off.

"Shit," Fargo swore as the sound reverberated in the cavernous barn. The man lay on his back on the floor, the pitchfork handle quivering in the air. Fargo leaped over him to get to the gun that had skittered a few feet away. He started to reach for it when two shots slammed into the wood floor only inches from his arma. He flung himself backward against one of the stacks of dried meat and saw the man who had stepped from behind the stacks at the other end of the barn.

The man was running toward him, firing too hastily, his shots close but missing. But there was no chance to reach the gun, Fargo saw. He only had the chance to fling himself into the narrow passage between the stacks. He grabbed the handle of the pitchfork as he did and yanked the implement

133

along with him. The man had seen which passageway he'd run into. He'd be at it pouring bullets down it in seconds, Fargo knew. Still holding the pitchfork, he grabbed on to one of the thick slabs of meat with his other hand and pulled himself up. Pushing with his feet, he clambered onto the top of the meat.

The man had reached the passage and Fargo heard him running down it. He was passing only a few feet below. Fargo leaned over and flung the pitchfork downward, a two-handed throw. The implement slammed into the figure as it passed, the center prong going through the back of the man's neck, the other two prongs sliding along both sides of his neck, as though they were there to keep his head in position. He fell forward onto his face. Fargo was about to jump down to get his gun when two more shots rang out, both slamming into the slab of meat where he stood. He saw the two men running toward him—one close to the passage-way, the other coming from the left side.

"Shit," Fargo swore as he leaped from the top of the stack to one on the other side and down, once more unable to reach a weapon. But he had taken care of two. However, he hadn't even the pitchfork now, and the two men were moving in on him. His only chance was to shake them, confuse them for a few minutes at least. He raced down the passage between the stacks, raced down another, turned and ran along at the rear of the barn where the stacks ended. He ran back and forth between the stacks, making no attempt to be quiet. Finally, he dropped to one knee and drew in a deep breath as he listened to the two men running back and forth to find him.

"He's over here, dammit," one shouted.

"No, I heard him run this way," the other called back.

Fargo smiled. They'd pull themselves together soon enough, he knew, settle themselves down to a more methodical search. His eyes swept the barn, seeking anything else he could use as a weapon. But he found nothing. The pitchfork appeared to have been the only implement in the barn. He had reduced the odds to two-to-one but that was still too much. He needed a gun. But only the thick slabs of dried meat looked mockingly down at him from their stacks. He felt the frown suddenly sliding across his forehead as his eyes stayed on one of the nearest stacks. Each slap of meat was wide and thick—almost a foot-and-a-half thick—but still solid and thicker than a man's body. The thought took shape as he stared at one slab. It was thick enough to easily absorb the bullets from a six-gun, even fired at close range.

He stood up, excitement surging through him and he reached up and tugged at the top slab on one of the stacks. It hardly budged. Bracing his foot against the stack, he pulled with all his strength. It came down this time, but heavier than he'd expected and slipped through his arms to drop onto the floor with a dull but definite thud. He heard the nearest searcher instantly change direction and start toward him. Fine, Fargo grunted. He wanted the man racing at him, anyway. He lifted the thick slab of meat. Christ, it was heavy, he thought. He held it up in front of him where it covered his torso from neck to waist. The man's racing footsteps were at the corner of the nearest stack.

Taking a firmer hold of his strange shield, Fargo leaped out with a shout as the man charged around the corner of the stack. He raced directly at the man who reacted instantly, firing his gun as fast as he could pull the trigger. Fargo felt the impact of the bullets as they slammed into the thick slab of meat. His meaty shield absorbed and stopped the slugs. He was driving forward as the man emptied his gun. He heard the click of the hammer on an empty chamber. The man tried to spin away. He was too late, as Fargo slammed into him with the extra weight of the thick slab.

The man went down as though he'd been hit by an onrushing buffalo. Fargo let the slap of meat drop on the man as he scooped up the gun and crashed the butt of it into his head for good measure. It had worked. He bent down for the cartridges to refill the gun. But he halted, disbelief sweeping through him. It couldn't be, he told himself. Yet it was, and he cursed softly. The man wasn't wearing a cartridge belt. Fargo's curses grew louder. He'd finally gotten hold of a gun, only it was empty and useless. He drew back behind the nearest stack.

The last of the searchers had halted. He was nearby, listening. He'd heard no cry of triumph after the fusillade of shots. He had to know something had gone wrong. Maybe he was smart enough to be scared. Or to panic and run. Fargo decided to find out. "Just you and me now," he called out. "You and me." He fell silent, waiting and picked up the faint sound of the figure moving between the stacks, going toward the front of the barn and the door. Maybe he was frightened enough to plain run, Fargo pondered. It wouldn't surprise him. The man had seen the odds go from five-to-one to even. He had to be scared. Fargo began to move forward between the stacks when he heard the man call out.

"Come out, your goddamn hands up," he said.

"Come get me," Fargo returned.

"Come out or I put a bullet in each of their damn heads," the man said and Fargo froze in his tracks.

"Damn," Fargo swore aloud softly. The man had become wily as a cornered rat, his move unexpected. A mistake, Fargo grimaced. Always a mistake to underestimate the desperate.

"I'm counting to ten," the man called. "You show or they get it."

No empty talk, Fargo realized. The man would play out his threat. He'd nothing to lose. The first shot might even bring his enemy running. Shit, Fargo swore. He'd brought down four of them in quick and bloody strikes only to be reduced to this. And still without a weapon. "One," the man began. "Two. Three."

Fargo began to walk toward the front of the barn. His eyes

scanned the floor as he passed the last row of stacks but there was nothing except sawdust there. Suddenly he halted. Sawdust, he bit out silently, a last, desperate chance. But then most last chances were desperate, he reminded himself. He knelt down, scooped up a handful of the sawdust and closed it in his fist and continued the last few steps between the stacks. "Seven. Eight," the man had called out when Fargo stepped into the open.

He saw the man, a thin-faced, slim figure, standing before Bonnie and Mary, a Smith & Wesson five-shot in his hand. Fargo walked forward slowly, his hands upraised and saw the man's eyes take in his belt and empty holster. "Looks like you win," Fargo said and slowly let his arms lower. "You're smarter than the others." He stepped closer, using slow, almost casual steps. "Let them go," he said with a nod toward Bonnie and Mary.

"You crazy?" the man said. "Why'd I do that?"

"Because you can keep me for Rossand," Fargo said. "That's the only thing that'll keep him from shooting your head off."

The man's thin face frowned at him. "What are you talking about?" he growled.

"I'm talking about what'll happen when Rossand comes back and finds the five of you couldn't keep me tied and then couldn't keep me from killing four of you," Fargo said and slid another step closer to the man. "You're going to be just one more stupid ass not worth keeping alive. But if I'm alive and tell him how the others screwed up and you were the only one with any brains, he just might keep you alive."

The man frowned at him, but Fargo could see the thoughts racing through his head. "I'll keep you and them," he said.

"No. They go or I don't talk for you," Fargo said and took a last half step forward. He was well within range, the sawdust burning inside his clenched fist now at his side.

The man stared at him, thoughts still churning inside his head. "I'll kill all three of you. Rossand won't care," he said.

"You're right, he won't. But he'll still kill you. I'm your only chance, sonny," Fargo said with reasonable logic coloring his voice. "You just going to kill these two lovelies in cold blood?" he said. "Look at them."

The man's eyes went to Mary and Bonnie and Fargo's arm came up and his hand flung the sawdust with the speed of a rattler's stroke. "Shit," the man half cursed and half coughed as the sawdust hit his face. Instinctively, he turned away, his eyes closed for a second. Fargo's blow caught him in the back of the neck and he flew forward to hit the floor on his hands and knees. He tried to turn, his eyes still blinking with sawdust in them and his hand came up to fire the gun. Fargo's kick sent the weapon spinning out of his hand and the man fell back and rolled. He shook his head as he pushed to his feet. He blinked away the remains of the sawdust, and saw the big man confronting him. He whirled and dived for the gun on the floor.

Fargo leaped forward, but the man reached the gun first. He scooped it into his hand and whirled and fired. The shot was too hasty. Fargo felt it graze his shoulder. Then he was closing with the man, wrapping his hand around the man's wrist. The man fired again and this time Fargo felt the heat of the bullet pass his cheek. He twisted the man's wrist, forced his hand downward. The man's finger tightened on the trigger again—probably inadvertently, Fargo realized.

The gun fired and the slim figure went limp. Fargo stepped back and the man crumpled to the ground, a red stain instantly widening across his midsection.

Fargo turned away from him and crossed to where Joey still lay with the hilt of the knife protruding from his chest. Fargo pulled the blade out, wiped it clean on Joey's sleeve and then cut Bonnie and Mary loose. Bonnie put her arms around him, a wordless embrace and then stepped back. He saw Mary slowly flexing the fingers of her hand. "They'll come back. Give them a few hours," he said.

He strode from the barn into the night, pausing to scan

the spread and saw the Ovaro tethered with the Appaloosa and Mary's horse. A small building that seemed an office stood nearby and he strode into it. He found he was right as he lit a kerosene lamp and saw the desk and file cabinet. He also saw what he had really come to find—his Colt hanging on the wall along with Mary's and Bonnie's guns.

They were both at the horses when he went outside and gave them their guns, his own comfortably back in its holster. "Let's ride," he said and they nodded despite the drained weariness in their faces.

He rode not more than a mile and found a cluster of red cedar to bed down in. Mary and Bonnie slept against him again, one on each side of him and he welcomed the restorative powers that only sleep could bring. He slept soundly to wake with the new sun and once again gently removed arms from around him. He used his canteen to wash. He was dressed and kneeling a dozen yards from the trees when Mary and Bonnie came over to him. He gestured to the deep tracks of the wagon. "They'll be easy enough to follow," he commented. "They'll be moving so slow, I'd guess we'll reach wherever they're going at the same time they will."

"What do you think we'll find?" Bonnie asked.

"I don't know," Fargo frowned. "But whatever it is, we're going to be careful. No mistakes, this time."

She nodded and he rose and climbed onto the Ovaro with a glance at Mary. "How are the fingers?" he asked.

"Much better," she said. "Good enough to pull a trigger."

He nodded and sent the pinto alongside the deep tracks of the wagon. The final chapter lay ahead. Maybe.

9

The land stayed fairly flat, ample tree cover but also plenty of wide, open space for wagons. Fargo set a fast pace and the day began to move into midafternoon when he halted and swung to the ground beside the wagon tracks. The soil was moist, freshly pressed down. "They're damn close," he said as he remounted and followed the trail that began a long, slow curve to the west. A thin line of box elder stretched alongside the wheel marks and he moved into the trees, Mary and Bonnie close at his heels. They'd ridden perhaps another mile when some structures took form just ahead. His eyes narrowed as he saw the wooden stockade fence with a wide double gate.

Inside the stockade he saw some five buildings—a barracks, stables, what seemed to be a warehouse and two smaller structures. Figures in blue uniforms with gold trim moved back and forth, some standing at ease at the double gate. He took in something else. Rossand's six big drays inside the stockade. "An army post," he heard Mary breathe.

"No, a line fort. Not even a major command post," Fargo said. "It's an army depot with a field unit attached."

"There's Rossand," Mary said. "He's dealing with the army."

"Seems that way," Fargo agreed as he watched an officer wearing captain's bars with a sheaf of documents in his hand standing beside Rossand. Fargo moved closer through the trees and came to a halt almost opposite the depot gate. The captain bent over and put his signature on two of the documents and handed one back to Rossand.

"The army just bought six wagonloads of beef and got three-quarters horsemeat. I'd say the army has been cheated," Bonnie observed.

"Probably for a long time," Fargo said and saw the drivers still sitting on the big drays. As he watched, a dozen troopers rode up to halt alongside the wagons.

"They're going to pull out," Mary said.

"With an army escort," Fargo said, his eyes on a young lieutenant at the head of the troopers.

"Let's stop them. We've got Rossand red-handed, his wagons filled mostly with horsemeat," Bonnie said.

Fargo's eyes held on the army captain for a moment as he let thoughts race through his mind before answering. "No, not yet. I want to find out where those wagons are going," he said. "I'm going to follow them. Rossand isn't going along. He'll be heading back to his place."

"We have to stop him now, with all the evidence right there," Bonnie insisted.

"After I find out where the wagons are going. They're getting ready to pull out now," Fargo said. "Soon as I've gone after them, you two go down to the captain. Tell him what you know. Tell him you can prove it. Tell him you want him to hold Rossand until I get there."

"All right. Rossand won't believe his eyes when he sees us," Mary said, excitement in her face and in Bonnie's. Fargo smiled. He knew they'd jump at the chance to confront Rossand. "One thing. Very important," Fargo said. "Don't tell anyone I've followed the wagons. Just tell them I'm on my way."

"All right," Mary said and Fargo's eyes went to the field depot where he saw the six wagons slowly moving out and turning southward. The escort of troopers split into two groups: one riding in front of the wagons, led by the young lieutenant, and the other falling in behind the last wagon.

A quick glance let him see Rossand and the captain walking into a low-roofed building, plainly the company quarters. He looked at Bonnie and Mary, his jaw suddenly tight.

"Give me ten minutes, then go to the captain," he said and they nodded, the excitement still in their faces.

He turned the Ovaro back to the rear of the trees and stayed behind the trees for almost a mile before he swung back and emerged. The wagons were a few hundred yards ahead, moving slowly and a quick glance at the sky told him there was perhaps another hour of daylight left. He hung back a while longer and fervently hoped he had made the right guess about the young lieutenant.

Bonnie walked the Appaloosa into the interior of the stockade, Mary beside her and both saw the glances of curiosity the passing troopers gave them. A corporal stepped forward as they halted in front of a small structure that bore the regimental pennant. "We want to see your commander," Bonnie said.

"That'd be Captain Tremont," the trooper said. "He has a visitor with him now."

"We know. We came to see him about that visitor," Mary said. "It'll be very important for him to see us." The corporal hesitated a moment, turned and disappeared into the building. He returned moments later.

"This way, ladies," he said and they followed him into a small office with a desk, a file cabinet and two straight-backed chairs. Rossand sat in one of them, turning to look at them as they entered. Bonnie gave him a big smile as she saw the astonishment flood his tight-skinned face. She almost laughed as his jaw dropped and he stared at her and Mary in utter disbelief.

Mary fastened her eyes on the captain and saw a tall man in a crisply pressed uniform, a hairline mustache and a face that carried a weak line to the mouth despite an aloof stare.

"Mary Keegan. This is my cousin, Bonnie Keegan," she said.

"You gave the corporal a very strange message, young ladies," Captain Tremont said. His aloof manner held an air of condescension in it, Mary decided. She turned a glare at Rossand, and held her eyes on him as she spoke to the captain. "So we did. Surprised, you stinking weasel?" she hissed at Rossand. He had recovered from his initial astonishment and she saw the cold glitter come into his eyes.

"You could say that," he answered evenly.

Her eyes stayed boring into Rossand, but her words went to the captain. "This man has been cheating the army for God knows how long," Mary said. "He just sold you six wagonloads of beef that is mostly horsemeat." She turned to see the captain look at Rossand, his eyebrows arching.

"These two young woman are mental cases, Captain. Everyone in the hill country knows it. They are always accusing people of wild things," Rossand said.

Mary and Bonnie exchanged glances that said the same thing. Rossand was hard to rattle. "A good liar gets lots of practice," Mary muttered.

"How long have we been doing business together, Captain?" Rossand asked with infuriating calmness.

"Four years. Since I was assigned this post," Tremont said.

"Have you ever found anything wrong with the beef I've brought you?" Rossand asked smugly.

"Never," the captain said.

"Have you ever examined it?" Bonnie cut in.

"Of course. Regulations insist we examine every shipment that arrives," the captain said.

"Have you ever looked below the top two layers?" Bonnie pressed.

"I don't remember everything we've done, but I just told you every shipment was checked," Tremont said with irritation in his voice.

"We can prove everything we've said. We're expecting someone else, a man named Fargo. We want you to hold Mister Rossand in custody until he gets here," Bonnie demanded.

Rossand rose, an almost sad smile on his wolfish face. "You know I've a busy operation to see to, Captain. I have to get back," he said.

"Lock him up, dammit," Bonnie insisted. "We'll prove everything when Fargo gets here."

Rossand's patient weariness stayed in his face. "These two are lunatics. They're on a campaign against me. Now they're trying to use the army to get their way. They're the ones who ought to be locked up."

"He's a cheating, thieving liar," Mary exploded.

The captain raised his voice. "Corporal," he called out and the soldier appeared at once. "Put these two young ladies in the guardhouse," Tremont said.

"What?" Bonnie and Mary chorused in unison.

"Take their guns," Tremont ordered.

"You can't do this. What's the matter with you?" Bonnie said as the trooper took their revolvers. "You've no grounds for this."

Tremont fastened a hard glare on both young women. "False accusations. Trying to use the United States Army for your own purposes. Making unsupported claims to an officer of the United States Army. Those will do for now," he said.

"This is crazy," Mary protested.

"You'll sit behind bars until this proof of yours arrives. If it doesn't, you'll stay behind bars," the captain said. "Take them away, Corporal."

"Dammit, you'll be sorry for this," Bonnie shouted at the officer as she was led from the office with Mary. A rifle-bearing trooper came up at once outside and strode beside them as the corporal led them to a small, square structure with a barred window.

"Inside," the corporal said as he opened the door to the guardhouse. Bonnie entered first, saw a second barred window at the back of the small room. Two cots and a washbasin took up two sides of the square room and a toilet hole on the other. The corporal pulled the door closed and spoke to them through the bars. "The trooper will be on guard outside the door all night," he said. "Not that you're going to get out but we don't take chances in the United States Army."

"You just put the wrong people in jail," Mary returned.

"I follow orders," he shrugged and strode away. Bonnie faced Mary's stare with her own shrug.

"I can't believe this," she said. "Dammit, this is Fargo's fault."

"Fargo's?" Mary frowned.

"Yes, if he'd gone down with us and faced Rossand in front of the captain with the wagons right there, it'd be over. Instead, he had to go off to see where the damn wagons were going," Bonnie said.

"So we wait till he gets here," Mary said.

"If nothing happens to him," Bonnie said and Mary's face reflected her own turbulent fears.

The dusk had begun to slide across the land when Fargo rode into the open and approached the line of wagons from the front. He slowed to a halt directly in front of them and saw the young lieutenant eye him cautiously. "I'd say you're the officer in charge here," Fargo remarked evenly.

"You'd say right, Mister. Lieutenant Evans," the young man said crisply.

"Could I have a word with you privately, Lieutenant?" Fargo asked.

The officer regarded him for a long moment, his young face serious. He motioned to two of his troopers and they followed as he sent his brown gelding a half-dozen yards away from the wagons. Fargo followed to halt beside him.

"This is as private as it's going to get, Mister," the lieutenant said.

"The name's Fargo, Skye Fargo," the Trailsman said. "You might have some trouble believing what I'm going to tell you, but I can prove everything I'm going to say."

"I'm listening," the young officer said.

"A question, first. Where are you going with these wagons?" Fargo asked.

"That's no secret. We're delivering this meat to three field stations. The army has the responsibility of delivering food to three of the southwest Indian tribes who'd made peace and agreed to stay on their reservations. The army doesn't allow them guns to hunt with so we have to deliver meat to them."

"Beef, I take it," Fargo said and the officer nodded.

"You had any troubles with the meat? Any complaints?" Fargo questioned.

Lieutenant Evans shot him a narrow glance. "There have been complaints from the tribes. There's also been an increase in sickness over the last few years," he said.

"What's the captain say about that?" Fargo asked.

"Captain Tremont feels the Indians are just complainers and their problems are brought about by their own bad hygiene and eating habits," Lieutenant Evans said.

"How do you feel about that, Lieutenant?" Fargo asked.

"I don't know. I've only been here six months," Evans said carefully.

"But you do know the Indians have existed well for hundreds of years with those bad hygiene and eating habits," Fargo said.

"I know that," Evans said uncomfortably. "I even mentioned that to the captain once. He told me I was too new out here to have opinions."

"You're carrying wagons loaded with three-quarters horsemeat, Lieutenant," Fargo said. "Much of it with whatever nutrition it might have had already lost. The army's been getting cheated and the Indians have been getting poor or even bad meat.''

Evans stared at him for a long moment. ''That's mighty big talk, Fargo,'' he said.

''The proof's right in those wagons. Take off the top two layers and you'll see,'' Fargo said. ''Go on, look for yourself.''

''All right,'' the young officer said after a moment.

''One thing more. Take most of your men to the side and tell them to be ready for trouble. Rossand's men on the wagons are going to know the game's over the minute you start taking off the top two layers of beef. They'll come up shooting to get away.''

The lieutenant nodded, turned to the two troopers and gave orders in a low, calm voice. Fargo followed along as the lieutenant returned to the wagons. He stayed back, watching most of the troopers draw to one side while four of the others began to pull the top layers of beef from the wagons. He watched Rossand's men exchange surprised glances at first, then nervous ones. Then he saw the panic of realization come into their eyes. The driver on the lead wagon was the first to turn panic into action as he yanked at his gun, drawing it up to fire at the lieutenant.

But Fargo's Colt was already in his hand and he fired. The driver toppled from the high seat as though he'd been blown off by a sudden gust of wind.

Instantly, the air was shattered with the sound of gunfire, the heavier boom of rifle shots predominant and Fargo saw Rossand's men falling from the wagons, some leaping down and twisting as bullets slammed into them in midair. Three had reached the ground and were on their knees waving their hands in the air.

''Cease fire,'' the lieutenant called and the dusk grew silent at once. He rode the brown gelding forward to the first two wagons where the top layers of beef had been pulled to the ground. He used his own rife to poke at the horsemeat, rode slowly along the side of the next wagon and finally turned back to where Fargo waited. "A lot of people will be thanking you, Fargo," he said. "Most won't even know you."

"A lot, but not everybody," Fargo answered.

"I'll be returning these wagons to the post," Evans said as night descended.

"I'll be riding on ahead of you," Fargo said, and the young officer nodded gravely. Fargo wheeled the Ovaro and put the horse into a gallop at once.

Mary and Bonnie sat curled up on the two cots, Mary with her eyes closed and her head back against the wall of the cell, Bonnie staring at the floor. The sound of the key in the door snapped them both to attention and they leaped to their feet. Captain Tremont entered, the guard at his side. "You two young ladies are very fortunate," the captain said.

"Fargo got here," Mary beamed.

"No," Tremont said. "I rather doubt there is any such person."

"Dammit, of course there is," Bonnie snapped.

"No matter. Mister Rossand came back. He said he really felt sorry for you both and that you needed a doctor's help. He asked that I release you in his custody. He'll take you back where you can get help. I agreed, of course, you'll be shackled but still, most men wouldn't be so understanding."

"You can't do that," Mary said in alarm.

"Do what?"

"Release us in his custody."

The captain gave them a slightly chiding smile. "First you object to being put in my jail and now you object to being released. Oh, my, you do need help," he said.

"He'll kill us," Bonnie said. "You're playing right into his hands."

"Mr. Rossand is going to eat, feed his horse and in an hour you'll be released in his custody. You ought to be grateful," Tremont said and strode from the cell. Bonnie thought that the sound of the key locking the door was the sound of doom.

"We're dead if Fargo doesn't get back damn soon," she cried out as she flung herself on the cot.

Mary settled down in grim silence on the other cot and a blanket of depression drew itself around both of them. It grew tighter as the minutes ticked steadily away. The end of the hour was drawing fatefully near. It was Mary who first heard the faint scraping sound at the rear window of the cell. She sat up, got to her feet and Bonnie came alert. Mary went to the window where, standing on tiptoe, she could see over the stone ledge. She peered into the night and the tall figure took shape alongside the back wall of the cell.

"Listen to me," the voice said.

"Jesus, what took you so long?" Mary breathed.

"How'd you know we were here?" Bonnie whispered.

"A sparrow told me. Cut the damn questions," he said and whispered instructions. Mary nodded and both stepped back from the window. Mary hurried to the door. She pounded on it and heard the guard's voice.

"What is it?" he asked.

"Something's wrong with my friend. I can't wake her up," Mary called and stepped back. The key turned in the lock and the trooper stepped into the cell, the rifle in hand. His eyes went to the limp form stretched on the floor near the cot.

"Get back," he said to Mary as he moved toward Bonnie. Mary stepped against the wall as the guard started to bend over Bonnie. He neither heard not saw the big man who silently stepped through the open door, but he felt the blow of the gun butt that crashed down on his head. He pitched forward, unconscious, as Bonnie rolled to one side and got to her feet.

"You'll never believe what happened," Bonnie said. "The captain believes Rossand, puts us in here and now he's about

150

to release us in Rossand's custody. How stupid can one man be?''

"He's not stupid,'' Fargo said, his voice tight and he saw Mary and Bonnie staring at him.

"Then he's the most gullible man I've ever seen,'' Mary said.

Fargo's face stayed hard. "He's neither stupid nor gullible. That's why I didn't want to confront Rossand with you. I didn't want to wind up in here with you,'' Fargo said. "I suspected exactly this would happen.''

"Why?'' Bonnie asked.

"Rossand's men have been delivering this fake beef for four years. In all that time a thorough inspection of the wagons would have been made at least once. But it never happened,'' Fargo said.

Bonnie's face filled with awe. "Because Tremont was in on it,'' she breathed.

"Bull's-eye. I figured Rossand couldn't have gotten away with it this long if there wasn't somebody working with him on the inside and that had to be somebody high up. Somebody who could see that there were never any real inspections.''

"Good God,'' Mary muttered.

"That's another reason I went after the wagons. I wanted to let the lieutenant see the truth for himself,'' Fargo said. "Let's go,'' he added and stepped to the door. He paused, glancing out across the darkened yard. It was quiet, with only the two troopers at the still open gates. Fargo crossed the space, Mary and Bonnie at his heels. He was almost to the captain's office when he saw the first wagon come into view, moving toward the stockade gate. He saw the lieutenant and two of his men riding ahead of it and he smiled as he halted outside the captain's door.

"There's usually a corporal here,'' Mary whispered.

"His shift's probably over for the night,'' Fargo said, closed one hand around the door and pushed it open. Captain

Tremont looked up in surprise from behind his desk, his eyes fastening on Bonnie and Mary first.

"Thought we'd save you the trouble of coming to get us," Mary smiled.

The man's eyes went to Fargo. "One shot and every man on my post will be here. I assure you they'll believe whatever I tell them," he said.

"Not anymore," a voice said and Fargo moved aside as the lieutenant came in with two of his troopers, his army-issue revolver in his hand. "Put the captain in irons," he ordered and the two soldiers obeyed at once.

"Your career's over, Mister," Tremont said. "You've no charges and no proof."

"I've got the charges. Dereliction of duty. Working with a civilian to defraud the United States Government. Betraying the uniform. Conduct unbecoming an officer," Evans said.

"You won't be able to make it stick," Tremont said, but Fargo noted he had lost the sneer in his voice.

"Six wagons outside will make it stick. My observations since I've been here will make it stick. And I'm sure Mister Rossand will talk to avoid a rope around his neck," Evans said.

"Rossand!" Fargo bit out. "He had to see you come back. He'd know what that meant. He's lit out by now."

"I'll send a detachment after him," the lieutenant said.

"A detachment won't catch him," Fargo said. "I'll go after him."

"We'll go after him," Bonnie said.

"I need you two here. I need to take depositions from you with all the details, everything you learned," Evans said.

"Stay here with the lieutenant," Fargo said and spun out of the room before they could protest further. He vaulted onto the Ovaro and paused at the gate. "A man ride out of here hell-bent for leather?" he asked the two sentries.

"Yes. Rossand, the one who supplies the meat," one of the sentries said. "He went north."

"Thanks," Fargo called back as he put the pinto into a gallop. He didn't bother to look for tracks. Rossand would be fleeing, riding as fast as he could across the plateau. He'd be racing for his place. It was almost certain he had his money hidden there someplace. Fargo sent the Ovaro full out across the flat land, skirting the tree clusters under an almost full moon. He'd rode hard for at least two hours when he saw the horse and rider ahead to his left and he shifted direction. He came up toward Rossand from the side and saw the man's horse was breathing hard, its strides shortening.

Rossand saw him suddenly, swerved and headed for a forest stand of oak and box elder. But Fargo was at his heels as he reached the trees. It would have been easy to blast him from his horse, but Fargo wanted him alive, if possible, so the lieutenant could use him against Tremont. Rossand had to slow when he entered the woods and he half turned to see Fargo close behind him. Rossand drew his gun, fired two shots that missed, veered through an opening between two oaks and fired again. This shot came closer, but still missed. Fargo pushed the Ovaro harder and the horse closed fast, racing up on Rossand's trail. Rossand spun in the saddle, taking a moment to aim this time and fired another shot. But Fargo was ready and he flung himself low across the horse's neck and heard the shot whistle over him.

He pushed himself up, only a few feet behind Rossand now. The man turned again, fired two more shots too quickly. They would have missed even if Fargo hadn't swung himself low against the side of the Ovaro. They were the last rounds in his gun, Fargo knew. He pulled himself up into the saddle and sent the Ovaro crashing forward. He came alongside Rossand and dived sideways, slamming into the man and went over the other side of the horse with him. He hit the ground atop Rossand and heard the man's gasp of pain. He pushed back, saw Rossand start to rise and saw the hunting knife he'd pulled from his waist. Rossand charged and Fargo waited, measuring split seconds and flung himself to one side as the knife all but grazed his shoulder. He landed on his back even as he was drawing the Colt. Rossand spun, charged at him again and Fargo fired from a prone position. He fired low and the bullet smashed into the man's kneecap.

Rossand fell with a scream of pain, the knife slipping from his hand as he clutched at his knee and rolled in agony. "Oh, Jesus," he groaned and Fargo got to his feet and stepped to him.

"Remember you said you got very displeased with people who try to stop you from earning a living?" Fargo remarked, then smiled. "Me, too." The Colt barked again and Rossand's other kneecap disintegrated in a shower of blood and bone.

"Aiiieeee, Jesus, oh, Jesus," Rossand screamed. Fargo holstered the Colt, reached down and took the man by the back of his shirt collar and dragged his screaming form to his horse. He lifted Rossand and threw him face down across his saddle.

"You might just be famous yet," Fargo said to him as he climbed onto the Ovaro. "You might be the first man hung from a wheelchair."

He started back, leading the other horse behind him and ignored Rossand's moaning sounds. He rather enjoyed them, he admitted to himself.

10

It was near the end of dusk and on the hill overlooking Horace Gregory's ranch, Fargo sat quietly on the Ovaro, Mary and Bonnie flanking him. Rossand had been left in Lieutenant Evan's custody and taken to an army hospital. The army would hold its own trial for Captain Tremont and a new supplier for beef had already been contacted. That left Horace Gregory, and Bonnie and Mary had insisted on returning with him.

"To us, he's the real bastard," Mary had said and she repeated the thought as Fargo stared down at the ranch below. "He's worse than Rossand. He supplied all those beautiful horses and knew what would happen to them. Without him, Rossand wouldn't have been in business."

"He's got a dozen horses down there now," Bonnie said.

"And almost as many men," Fargo grunted.

"Hired hands. Small-timers. Gregory done in, they'll run, each man for himself. They won't want to be around to answer questions," Bonnie said.

"I say get the federal marshal and let him make the arrest and you testify," Fargo said.

"It'll take too long. Gregory will hear about Rossand by then. He doesn't know yet. He'll take off, go somewhere and find another Rossand someplace," Mary said.

"Thta's not going to happen," Bonnie said, ice in her voice.

"Besides, prison wouldn't be enough. Neither would

hanging," Mary said equally icy. "There's no justice in either of them. Not the right kind."

"He's got a compound of fine dogs down there. I'd hate to see anything happen to them," Fargo said.

"So would we. I'm sure Will Stedman could use them. They'd come in real handy for herding in his operation," Mary said. "We might take in a couple."

Fargo looked from one to the other. "Got everything figured out, haven't you," he said and they nodded as one. "What's my part?"

"We wait till everyone's asleep. Then you go down with us, but we'll go to the main house and you go to the corral," Mary said. "You wait there, give us five minutes, then open the corral door and stampede the horses."

"That'll mean shots," Fargo said.

"That's all right. It'll be done with by the time the men get their pants on," Mary said. "You stampede the horses and leave the rest to us."

"You expect Gregory will come running outside at the sound of the horses and you'll be there waiting to cut him down," Fargo said.

There was no denial, he noted and he swung from the horse and sat down against a tree. "It'll be a while. I'm going to rest some. It'll keep me from thinking about what you two oughtn't to be doing," he said. He still received no answer and he closed his eyes and let himself relax as the night came. He understood their feelings, from the head as well as the heart. But he didn't want to see them get hurt at the last moment, after all they'd done to pursue the truth of it. Yet they'd earned their right to justice as they saw it. He'd play his role. They deserved that.

He dozed, letting the night grow longer and when he woke the third time, he rose to his feet to see Bonnie and Mary on their mounts. He climbed onto the Ovaro and started down the hillside with them. The ranch was dark and silent and they halted at the bottom of the hill, tethered the horses in the trees and moved the rest of the way on foot. He paused at the narrow roadway that led to the corral, saw the young women moving toward the main house on silent footsteps. He moved on. He reached the corral gate and dropped to one knee and began to count off seconds.

Bonnie and Mary opened the front door of the house with care, not making a sound. It took them only a moment to hear Horace Gregory's snores coming from the room at the end of the corridor. They hurried to it, entered and Bonnie went to one side of the bed and Mary the other. They drew their pistols, Mary pressing hers to the right side of Horace Gregory's temple, Bonnie to the left. The man's eyes popped open, grew wider. "Get up, you piece of shit," Bonnie hissed and kept her gun against the man's temple as he swung from the bed. He wore only underdrawers and his eyes shot gray-blue hate.

"You crazy bitches," he growled. "What do you think you're going to get away with?"

"Nothing," Mary said. "Walk." The man stumbled down the corridor, the two guns still against him. They took him from the house and Mary saw the hint of sudden fear in Gregory's quick glance.

"What do you want? I'm a reasonable man," he said.

"Good," Mary said as they reached the roadway in front of the house. "Sit down," she ordered.

"Go to hell," Gregory rasped. Bonnie's gun butt came down across the side of his temple, not hard enough to knock him unconscious but hard enough to send him to the ground. Mary yanked the length of the lariat from the pocket of her Levis, dropped to one knee and had Horace Gregory's ankles bound loosely together before he could clear his head. Bonnie reached down and together they lifted the man to his feet.

"Goddamn, what do you want?" Gregory barked as they dragged him to the center of the road and flung him to the ground. He looked up and saw Mary frowning at Bonnie. "It's time, dammit," he heard her hiss. Suddenly, not more than ten seconds later, shots exploded in the silence of the night. They were almost drowned out by the wild snorts and the thunder of hooves pounding into the ground. He saw Mary and Bonnie racing away and then he turned, saw the mass of horses racing toward him. His mouth opened, flinging curses soundlessly. He pushed to his feet, tried to run and fell. He tried to crawl, hands clawing desperately into the ground. He turned and screamed as the flying hoofs rose up over him.

Fargo was on his feet, holstering his Colt as the horses charged from the corral, a black cloud of thundering bodies. He heard the scream, Gregory's voice, almost unrecognizable with the terror in it. The scream came again, all but drowned out by the thundering of the stampeding horses and then there was only the sound of hoofbeats fading into the night. He walked across the road and into the trees. It seemed as though Bonnie and Mary had waited for the noise of the stampede and his shots to cover their own. He frowned and walked on, not satisfied with what seemed.

The shouts of the men emerging from the bunkhouse were distant. And totally unimportant. He found the Ovaro standing alone, climbed into the saddle and sent the horse up the hillside at a walk. When he reached the top he saw the other two horses, Bonnie and Mary standing beside them. "Thought you'd be here," he said, peering hard at them. Both their faced were calm. Maybe with the hint of quiet triumph, he mused. "You finished him?" he asked.

"No, not us," Mary said. "Not us." They smiled, a private exchange and suddenly he understood. There were many roads to justice.

11

He'd spent the day relaxing at the house in the hollow and had gone into Hillsdale for a sack of salt Mary wanted. He'd stopped at the dance hall and Patty greeted him with a kiss and a squeal of delight. The bartender nodded at him. The wiry figure with the derby hat and red bow tie wasn't at his usual place at the corner of the bar. Some of the other girls came up as Patty read the question in his eyes.

"He's gone," she said. "We own the place now. All of us. We run it, share the expenses and split the take."

"Congratulations," Fargo said. "You buy out McAdoo?"

"Not exactly," Patty said.

"We told him we knew how he'd been ready to let any of us be killed," one of the other girls said. "We told him he'd be smart to sell out to us."

"He didn't seem the kind to take advice," Fargo said.

"He wasn't, but sometimes fate plays a part," Patty said. "You've a free pass any time you want, Fargo."

"I'll remember that," he said and Patty gave him another hug before he left. He paused outside where a weathered old man held a broom in hand. "Heard about McAdoo leaving," Fargo said. "You know where he went?"

"They found him at the bottom of a gulch, head split open by the rocks. Seemed he fell from his horse and went to the bottom," the old man said.

"He wasn't shot or anything," Fargo pressed.

"Nope," the man said. "One funny thing, though. He had

one of those net stockings the girls wear stuffed into his mouth. Nobody could explain that."

"Fate gets a little help sometimes," Fargo said as he walked away.

He rode back to the hollow with Mary's sack of salt. Horace Gregory's men had fled the place and the dogs were taken by Will Stedman. Except for one border collie and one Bernese that Mary and Bonnie took. Fargo stretched out on the small porch in front of the house. It was time to move on. He'd tell Mary and Bonnie in the morning and leave them to their causes and their world. The sun was beginning to dip behind the hills when Bonnie came out to him, sat down close beside him.

"I want you to do something for me, Fargo," she said. "You know how I told you Mary always hangs back with men. I got her to agree not to do that with you."

"No kidding?" Fargo said, summoning instant surprise.

"She needs someone like you to help her enjoy herself for once. She's agreed to go to your room tomorrow night," Bonnie said and Fargo knew Mary had to have had trouble keeping her air of reluctance. "Of course, she doesn't know about the night we had. She'd back off if she did," Bonnie said.

"It'll be our secret." Fargo smiled and Bonnie nodded, honestly happy as she hurried back into the house. The darkness was starting to pull itself around the hills when Mary came out.

"Supper will be ready soon," she said and knelt down beside him. "Do a favor for me, Fargo?" she asked.

"Why not?" he returned.

"I told you how Bonnie comes on a little strong with men. She held back with you, mostly because she knew I'd disapprove. That wasn't right of me and I know she wants you. She mentioned she might come visit you night after tomorrow. Do right by her, Fargo. She deserves the pleasure."

"If you say so," he agreed with just the right note of humbleness.

"Of course, she doesn't know about us . . . about that night. She wouldn't go to you if she did. She'd feel she was intruding on me," Mary said.

"It'll be our secret," Fargo said and Mary brushed his cheek with her lips as she happily hurried back into the house. Fargo let a sigh escape him as he leaned back. He'd have to stay a little longer. Doing good deeds was a man's duty. So was keeping secrets.

They were still a strange pair. But they looked out for each other. They cared about each other. He could do no less. Nobility had its rewards, he thought smiling in happy anticipation.

LOOKING FORWARD!

**The following is the opening
section from the next novel in the exciting
Trailsman series from Signet:**

THE TRAILSMAN #125
BLOOD PRAIRIE

*1860—on the long, hard trail
between the Kansas Territory and
the booming town of Denver,
a trail littered with the bones
of those who died along the way.*

The blizzard swept out of the west with all the fury of a rampaging grizzly bear.

An hour before, the big man had been riding westward across the plains of Kansas at an easygoing pace, his magnificent Ovaro stallion covering the miles effortlessly. The superbly muscled forms of both the rider and the horse flowed together in perfect coordination. Here was a man born to the saddle and a horse with all the spirit and stamina of a wild mustang. They were part and parcel of the endless tract of grassland surrounding them, as at home on the plains as the buffalo and the coyote.

Excerpt from BLOOD PRAIRIE

The big man's penetrating lake-blue eyes had narrowed when the roiling bank of slate gray clouds first appeared on the horizon and came directly toward him. He'd straightened, inhaling the crisp, cool air deeply, and shifted to survey the grassland on both sides. Nowhere was there a place to take shelter, not even so much as a sparse stand of trees, and he'd urged the stallion to go faster.

Now, an hour later, he still sought a spot to sit out the inevitable storm. A lifetime spent in the wild enabled him to read the weather like most men could read a book, and he knew the recent snap of unseasonably mild January weather was about to take a dramatic turn for the worse. By next morning the plains would likely be buried under a foot or more of snow.

The prospect of heavy snow didn't worry him. He'd lived through snowstorms before and would do so again. His saddlebags contained plenty of jerked beef, coffee, and other victuals, so he wouldn't starve should game prove difficult to obtain. More worrisome was the drop in temperature. Already the temperature must have plunged ten degrees, and by nightfall it would undoubtedly hover near zero or below.

Skye Fargo glanced up at the thick blanket of clouds blotting out the entire sky and frowned. Soon the flurries would commence and he had yet to find a place to hole up in. He was scores of miles from the nearest settlement and the closest fort lay hundreds of miles away. There might be an Indian village in the general vicinity but, if so, it was probably Cheyenne and some of the young bucks had been kicking up their heels lately, waylaying unwary travelers. He wouldn't feel very safe staying with them.

Unfortunately, the grasslands of Kansas were as flat as a plate. Not without reason had they once been widely known as the Great American Desert. Adequate natural shelters were few and far between. Much farther west, along the foothills of the Rockies, and back east in the forested tracts of

Missouri, there were plenty of places to take shelter from the elements. Not so in Kansas—unless a man could burrow into the ground like a prairie dog.

Ten minutes later the snow began. Initially, the few flakes were small and fluttered to the earth in the stiff breeze. Gradually the size of the flakes increased and the trickle became a downpour.

Fargo twisted to untie the heavy sheepskin coat rolled up behind his saddle along with his bedroll. Donning the coat, he flipped the collar erect to ward off the flakes from his neck. He left the front of the coat unbuttoned to give him quick access to the Colt .44 strapped to his right hip. In addition to the revolver, he had a Sharps rifle snug in its saddle holster and a razor-sharp throwing knife in a sheath in his right boot. He was exceptionally adept with all three weapons and felt confident he could handle any trouble that came his way.

The snow whispered as it fell, a soft sigh much like that of a woman in a passionate embrace. Soon a thin white layer covered the ground and more piled on top with every passing second.

Fargo felt the wind pick up. Visibility was now restricted to under twenty yards, which made it difficult for him to spot a resting place. Having no other recourse, he forged onward, his shoulders hunched against the biting cold. The Ovaro's hoofs thudded dully on the ground, its breath issuing from its nostrils in smoky puffs.

In no time at all the plains had been transformed into a winter wonderland. The snow depth rose from an inch to two inches, then to three.

Fargo couldn't take his bearings by the sun and had no landmarks to rely upon. He counted on his unerring instincts to take him in the right direction. If a man lived in the wilderness long enough, he sometimes acquired the ability to figure out which way was which by relying on a sort of sixth sense, on a mysterious inner compass as reliable as any ever made. Many Indians had the knack, as did the old-time mountain men, and every scout worthy of the name had it too.

As one of the generally acknowledged top scouts in the West, Fargo seldom became lost. Even when in totally unfamiliar country, he invariably found his way around with an ease born of long experience. And it was safe to say that few living men had covered as much territory as he had. Kit Carson was one. The legendary Jim Bridger was another notable exception. Like them, he was a wanderer who couldn't abide staying in any one place very long. If he wasn't on the go, he wasn't happy.

Now though, Skye found himself wistfully wishing he'd stayed in Kansas City with Eleanor for a few more days. Cuddling with her wram, voluptuous body sure beat freezing his ass off in a blinding snowstorm any day of the week. Thinking of the way she had liked to sit astride him, bucking in pleasure until she was totally spent, brought a smile to his lips. She had been all woman.

The snowfall intensified, and Fargo could feel the clammy flakes sticking to his face and throat. He pulled his hat down tighter around his ears and his coat collar up higher. Tucking his chin to his chest, he rode ever westward. Time lost all meaning. He was aware of the plodding Ovaro and the falling snow and nothing else.

Much later, when he estimated sunset couldn't be more than an hour off and he had about resigned himself to making camp on the open prairie, he came on the tracks. Surprised, he drew rein and stared down at the freshly made wagon-wheel marks, unable to explain their presence.

Fargo, as was his habit, was well off the beaten path. Ten miles or more to his north was the rutted trail used by the majority of pilgrims heading through the Kansas Territory to the gold fields in the Rockies. Anyone traveling westward in a wagon would be bound to use that trail, if only because there were a few way stations along the route where a body could feed stock, rest, and enjoy a hot meal.

But right there, inches from the pinto's front legs, were the distinct tracks left by a number of wagons making to the southwest. Fargo leaned down to examine them closely. The edges were still clear, the bottom of the ruts hardly covered with snow, which indicated the wagons had passed this way less than fifteen minutes ago. Straightening, he gazed into the storm in the direction the wagons had gone. Where the hell were they going? he reflected. There was nothing out there except mile after mile of prairie. No towns. No settlements. No ranches or farms or anything.

It didn't make sense.

Fargo went to spur the Ovaro westward, then hesitated. What if those people were lost? What if they'd somehow strayed from the trail, then became disoriented in the storm? He figured there were six or seven wagons, judging from the tracks. There might be women and children on board. And since the storm had worsened to where it was almost a blizzard, those folks might find themselves in a lot of trouble come morning. He could be of help. But should he bother? After all, there might be a logical reason for the wagons being so far off the beaten track. Going after them could turn out to be a waste of time better spent seeking shelter from the snowstorm.

What should he do?

Fargo stared westward, then down at the wagon tracks. If there was one lesson every man who lived in the West learned sooner or later, it was to never meddle in the affairs of others. Sticking your nose in where it didn't belong could be downright dangerous. On the other hand, it was natural for strangers to offer a helping hand to anyone in need. That thought caused him to spur the Ovaro along the trail. He stayed to the left of the ruts, riding hard, eager to get it over with and be on his way if it should develop that he was on a fool's errand. Since he wasn't far behind the wagons, he'd overtake them in five or ten minutes.

The snow fell faster. The wind began to howl and whipped the flakes against his exposed skin, stinging him with tiny spears of fleeting pain. The cold worsened.

Fargo breathed shallowly to keep the searing cold out of his lungs. His nostrils tingled in the frigid air. He longed for a roaring fire to get his blood flowing again and a steaming cup of coffee to warm his insides. The tracks, thankfully, continued to be easy to read, the edges sharply defined, leading him to speculate that he was rapidly gaining ground. Moments later, in confirmation, a horse whinnied somewhere up ahead.

Skye squinted into the storm, seeking the wagons, and spied a large, vague shape at the limits of his vision. Slowing, he cupped his right hand to his mouth, about to call out and let them know he was friendly. The last thing he wanted was a nervous greenhorn taking a potshot at him. Suddenly, to his right, someone shrieked a single word.

"Indians!"

A gun boomed, and Fargo felt the slug tug at his hat. He shifted in the saddle, his right hand streaking toward his Colt, aware he was already too late. A lean figure launched itself from out of the white shroud and sinewy arms looped around his waist. The impact knocked him off the Ovaro, his attacker clinging to him as they fell.

Somewhere, there were loud shouts.

Landing hard on his right side, Fargo winced in pain. A fist slammed into his stomach but the blow, lacking strength, barely fazed him. He placed both hands on the shoulders of his attacker and shoved, tearing the man off and getting a good look at his face. That's when he discovered it wasn't a man. His attacker was a youth of fifteen or sixteen, no older.

"Indians!" the youth screamed. "Indians!"

Fargo saw the youth's eyes alight on his face, saw the shock of recognition as the tenderfoot realized he wasn't a red man after all, and then he delivered a punch of his own to the teenager's midsection, doubling the youth over. "I'm no Indian, you idiot," he snapped.

The youth gurgled and sputtered, his hat falling off as he thrashed his head from side to side. His face turned beet red.

Running feet pounded. Shadowy forms converged, attended by loud yells.

"What the hell is going on?"

"Where are the Indians?"

"Over this way!"

"It's the Tyler kid!"

Fargo stood, brushing snow off his clothes, and swung around to face the newcomers, who collectively drew up short in consternation. There were eight, all told, with more coming. The youth rose slowly to his knees and grabbed his fallen hat.

"Who are you, mister?" demanded a burly man in a fur-collared coat and a derby. In his right hand was a Smith and Wesson that he leveled at Fargo's gut.

"I don't like having hog-legs pointed my way," Skye said. "Put that away before I make you eat it."

"Now see here," chimed in a blond man wearing fancy store-bought duds. "We don't know who you are and we have no reason to trust you. For all we know, you might have been sneaking up on us to rob us."

"Yeah," added another belligerently. "Why else did you beat on the kid there?"

"I'm not a kid!" Tyler exploded angrily, rising with his fists clenched. "And I'll pound the next one who says I am."

For a second all eyes were on the youth, and Fargo instantly took advantage of the distraction by taking a quick stride and swatting the Smith and Wesson aside while simultaneously drawing his Colt and ramming the barrel into the burly man's abdomen. "I told you to put your hardware away,'' he growled, and cocked the Colt's hammer so everyone could hear it click. "I won't tell you again."

The burly man looked into Fargo's eyes and gulped. A strained silence descended as everyone froze. They were all apprehensive, fearing the gunshot they certainly believed would shatter the stillness.

"Hold on there, handsome," said a calm female voice in a decidedly friendly tone. "Pete is just looking out for our interests, is all. He doesn't mean any harm. Why, he's never shot so much as a rabbit with that piece of his."

Fargo glanced at the speaker, a shapely redhead in a gray dress and a black shawl, who was pressing through the group. "Pete doesn't listen very well," he commented, and reached out to pluck the Smith and Wesson from the man's unresisting fingers. Stepping back, he holstered the Colt and wedged the Smith and Wesson under his belt.

"Apparently we've gotten off on the wrong foot," the woman said, stopping right in front of him. She fearlessly studied his features, her own showing intense curiosity.

"You can say that again," Fargo said. "I came on your tracks a while back and figured I'd check to see if you folks needed help. The next thing I know, someone tries to blow my head off and Tyler here jumps me."

The redhead turned to the youth. "I thought I heard you shouting something about Indians."

Tyler frowned and averted his gaze. "I was keeping watch like Briggs wanted when I saw a horse and rider come out of nowhere. The snow's so thick I couldn't see all that well." He nodded at Fargo. "All I saw was buckskins, so I thought it must be Indians."

"Was that you who fired?" she inquired.

"Yep. Snapped off a shot without thinking," Tyler said sheepishly. "I'm really sorry, Molly."

"Don't tell me," Molly responded, and gestured at Skye. "He's the one you should be apologizing to."

"Sorry, mister."

Fargo's anger subsided. He couldn't stay mad at a green kid and a bunch of pilgrims who didn't have enough sense to find shelter out of the storm. "A man should always know what he's shooting at before he squeezes a trigger," he admonished the youth.

"It won't happen again," Tyler said.

"Where's your rifle?" Molly asked.

"I dropped it when I jumped the stranger," Tyler explained. "I knew I wouldn't have time to reload before he got off a shot, so I up and tackled him." He pivoted. "I'd better find that gun before the snow covers it." Off he went.

"My name is Molly Howard," the redhead revealed, and offered her right hand. "Who are you?"

"Skye Fargo," he answered, gently taking her palm in his. Her skin was pleasantly warm to the touch, her grip surprisingly firm. He noticed the way her bosom made the shawl swell outward and her attractively slim hips. "Pleased to make your acquaintance."

The man called Pete coughed. "We're getting set to pitch camp for the night, Mr. Fargo. You're welcome to join us if you want. I'm sure Buffalo Briggs won't mind."

"You're fixing to make camp *here*?" Fargo asked in disbelief, unable to conceive of anyone being so outright dumb.

"Close by," Pete said. "Buffalo Briggs says the storm will blow over in a couple of hours and we can resume our journey."

"Who is this Buffalo Briggs you keep talking about?"

"He's our wagon master."

From behind the onlookers, who now numbered sixteen people, came a stern voice. "Let me through, folks." The group parted to permit a tall, lanky man attired in buckskins and a fringed buckskin coat to advance. He wore a high white hat, a flowing red bandana, and white gloves. Strapped around his waist, outside the coat, were two nickel-plated, ivory-handled Colts. A flowing mustache and a neatly trimmed beard decorated his haughty face. "I'm George Briggs, but everyone calls me Buffalo Briggs because I spent time as a buffalo hunter before I took to guiding wagon trains for a living." He eyed Fargo critically. "I was up yonder, scouting for a spot to stop, when I heard a shot. Are you giving these fine folks grief? If you are, you'll have to answer to me."

Fargo bristled at the threat and went to answer, but the redhead beat him to the punch.

"This man didn't do anything except protect himself, Briggs. Tyler jumped him without provocation."

"I told the lad to be on the watch for savages, Miss Howard," the wagon boss said rather stiffly. "He was just doing his job. I can't fault him for that."

"Tyler is lucky Mr. Fargo didn't kill him," Molly said.

Briggs seemed to stiffen. "Who did you say?" he asked, glancing intently at Skye.

"Fargo. This gentleman's name is Skye Fargo," Molly elaborated. "Why? Do you know him?"

"I know *of* him," Briggs said, and he did not sound pleased although his mouth curved in a smile. He shoved his right hand out. "So you're Skye Fargo, the scout and Indian fighter. I've heard that you're almost as good as Kit Carson, and I'm honored to make your acquaintance, sir."

Puzzled by the man's behavior, Fargo shook.

"You're an Indian fighter?" Pete asked, and nodded at the wagon boss. "Then you must have heard all about Mr. Briggs. He killed Chief Gray Wolf and twelve Sioux at the battle of Webster Pass."

"Oh?" Fargo said.

"Yes, sir," Pete said, his chin bobbing in excitement. "We heard all about it in Kansas City. It's one of the reasons we hired him to lead us to Denver."

Buffalo Briggs cleared his throat. "I'm certain Mr. Fargo doesn't want to be bored listening to you relate my exploits,

Peter." He shifted and clapped his hands. "Now let's get back to our wagons, folks. I wasn't able to find any cover, so we'll make camp right here and wait for the snow to stop." He motioned for them to move off.

"What about you, Mr. Fargo?" Molly inquired. "Would you care to join us?"

"Yeah, please do," Pete added. "We'll need all the help we can get if any hostiles pay us a visit."

The wagon boss looked at him sharply. "We can handle any bucks hankering to give us trouble," he stated. "Fargo probably has business elsewhere and we don't want to detain him."

Skye saw both Molly and Pete stare at him expectantly. By all rights, given the manner in which he'd been treated so far, he should mount up and ride off. He owed these people nothing, and Briggs clearly didn't want his company. But he hesitated, his mind awhirl with questions. Who was this Buffalo Briggs? In all his years on the frontier, Skye had never heard of him. Nor had he ever heard about the battle of Webster Pass. He didn't even know of a pass by that name. His intuition told him something was wrong here, and his curiosity prompted him to find out what it was.

"Please join us," Molly stressed, and reached out to touch his forearm. "We'd be delighted to have you ride with us for as long as you want."

Briggs made an impatient gesture. "We don't want to impose on Mr. Fargo, my dear. He's a man of the open spaces and likes his privacy, I'd wager. If he'd rather go on, it's his affair."

The man's condescending attitude rankled Fargo. In fact, practically everything about Buffalo Briggs rubbed him the wrong way. He peered up into the swirling snow, which now qualified as a first-rate blizzard, and came to a decision. "I'd be happy to join you," he said.

Molly beamed, then brushed snow from her bangs. "I have hot coffee in my wagon if you'd care to join me."

"Much obliged," Fargo said, and walked to the Ovaro. He took the stallion's reins and waited for her to take the lead.

"Pardon me," Pete remarked. "Is there any chance I could have my gun back? I just bought it in Kansas City and I don't think I've fired it ten times."

"I don't see why not," Fargo said, forking the iron over. He trailed Molly toward the wagons, passing the wagon boss, and swore he could feel the man's eyes bore into his back. It was an uncomfortable sensation, as if he'd turned his back on a rattler coiled to strike.

What had he gotten himself into? he wondered.

JON SHARPE'S WILD WEST